Whisky for Breakfast

Whisky for Breakfast

Christopher P. Mooney

Bridge House

British Library Cataloguing in Publication Data
A Record of this Publication is available from the British
Library

ISBN 978-1-907335-89-1

This edition published 2020 by Bridge House Publishing
Manchester, England

In memory of my mother and brother.
And for my father.

You should be a poet, or a writer.
Lucy Cordery, January 2003

These words I write keep me from total madness.
Charles Bukowski

Contents

The Grey Shamus

I was wearing an open-neck black shirt under a charcoal suit that had seen more funerals than weddings on the late-summer day it all started, with the world around me wet from an unseasonal drizzle that had fallen overnight from a tornado-green sky. It was bright in spite of the damp and the day was full of promise. I had no way of knowing it was the beginning of a week that would etch itself forever in the cracks of my mind.

I watched through liver-sick eyes as the woman in the motel room with me, still soft and warm from bed, got back into her panties. Loose-limbed yet languid, with impossible tits, she moved with a grace that was almost feline. Truth be told, I had to resist the urge to start clapping.

'What time is it?' she asked, the words dripping from her tongue like syrup off a spoon.

'I don't know,' I said, because I didn't, and set fire to a cigarette; hoping it would dent the clawing sperm smell making the room stuffier than a busy launderette.

'Smoking's a filthy habit,' she said.

'I know,' I said, 'but I picked it up young so I reckon on keeping it.' A long, satisfying drag. 'And another thing: mind your business.'

A strange silence.

She noticed me staring at her. That look in my eyes.

I managed to keep my mouth shut.

I reached for the remote and switched on the tube above the bed. It was showing the races.

'You play the ponies?' she asked, pulling on a pair of blue jeans so tight they made me want to believe in God. Any god. Then the fuck-me pumps. A shadow of pride no doubt passed across my face as I reminded myself I'd spent half the night wearing her like a ham mask. For the record,

9

her vulva smelled like damp roses and tasted like salted caramel.

I nodded. 'Sometimes.'

'You win?'

'No,' I said, 'not even once. My luck's so bad, if it was raining pussy I'd get hit with a dick.'

'I'd rather be good than lucky.'

'I'd rather be lucky than lose,' I said. 'Besides, nobody ever does.'

'Nobody ever does what?'

'Win. Nobody wins.'

'How come?'

'Most of the tracks are loaded. Crooked gates, bent jockeys, doped mares, that sort of stuff. Even laced blinkers. The guy off the street who don't know nobody to throw him the skinny, his money's no longer his own before he even picks a seat in the grandstand, never mind picks a fucking horse. It's a real tough game. That's how come you never see a bookie on a bike.'

'That's too bad. It's awful they treat people that way.'

'How does your way of life treat you?'

'I get by, I suppose,' she said. 'Most of the johns treat me fair.'

'Really? I'm surprised,' I said, because I was.

'Yeah. Except one I had in here last night. A big, fat, sweating bastard of a man. He was so huge he could probably pick up a hippo with one hand. And put it in his shirt pocket.'

'That big, huh?'

'Absolutely. I never seen a person that size before. Like a G-Wagon with feet.'

'The only way I could afford a car like that would be if I lived in it,' I said. 'Did you happen to catch this guy's name?'

'Nah, he didn't throw it. Most of 'em don't, unless it's a phoney. How come?'

'No reason.'

'You know what he said to me?'

'I'm sure I don't.'

'He has this girl, he said, real young, and he asked if there might be a way to put her to work. You know, like what I do.' She paused, as if for emphasis. 'Can you fucking believe that?'

'Unfortunately, yes. Listen,' I said, reaching a hand inside my jacket, 'what name should I put on the cheque?'

'I suppose you think that's funny.'

'It has been.'

'What name do *you* use?'

'The one I was given,' I said. 'The only one I've got. It was the first and last thing my old man gave me.'

'Yeah?'

'Yeah.'

'How does it go?'

'Carmichael.'

'Carmichael? That's it? There ain't nothin' else?'

'That's right. Just Carmichael. It's all I need,' I said, figuring I didn't want to be on first-name terms with this kind of woman, no matter how good she looked with no clothes on.

I pulled three of the last four twenties out my wallet as I used my bulk to usher her toward the door. Because everybody knows you don't pay her for the sex; you pay her to leave afterward. I don't like getting it that way but, the state I'm in, they're the only answer I have to the insoluble question of insatiable need.

'This guy right here,' I said, pointing with my left to the money in my right, 'was the first Scotsman to appear on an English banknote.'

11

'Is that so? I never knew that.'

'No reason why you should.'

'How's that?'

'Because you're a hooker; and when you're a hooker, I imagine every day's a school day,' I spat through a mouthful of black laughter. More quick than clever but the best I could do with an itchy tongue and a thumping skull.

'Go fuck yourself,' she snarled.

'No need,' I said to her back, shooting my cuffs. 'So long, doll. And thanks.'

As soon as she'd gone, her departing syllables vibrating on every nerve, I put on my overcoat and headed downstairs. The rate paid up front, I ducked out past the desk and hit the street.

An old shuffling bum, eyes downcast and humble, made me for a smoke right off and I gave it to him and even lit it for him. The shy way he said thanks reminded me of Linda's soft voice.

Linda.

She was big, heavy but not fat, with no excess flesh covering her well-tanned, handsome frame. I was attracted to her, and felt good when she was around.

We'd got together thousands of miles ago when we thought we knew each other but didn't yet know ourselves. Urged on by a mutual need to be wanted and a common want to be needed, we clung to the small things we shared. We built sandcastles in the air on these short-term foundations; long-term, there was no better glue than habit and history. When it was good, it was fucking great. When it was bad, it was usually my fault. I didn't realise how lucky I was until too long after our clouds of happiness had burst, when moths were eating what remained of the matrimonial duvet.

She was troubled, with a long and sordid history of

substance abuse, I knew that, but she always said she didn't want anyone to try to fix her. And I always said I never would. I thought she was happy enough with what we had. Not so. After that last fight, she swore I'd never see her again and made damn sure I couldn't. I haven't had a word off her from that day to this and I know now I'll more than likely never see her again. I'll never be able to evict the hermetic memories of her from the rooms of my mind.

Linda. Jesus. A loss so complete it had shrunk the spleen. The shadow I cast hasn't changed but the truth of it is I've not been the same since.

The split hit her hard, too. Last I heard, she'd fallen back into a spiral of addiction. If she's not dead already, chances are she'll soon be nothing more than buried bones in borrowed black. Some would say when she was with me she was never anything else.

I knew it would be heroin and I knew where she'd be getting it from. That filthy prick. The number of lives he's ruined will never be counted and the damage can never be made right, no matter how many of his kind I put away or put down.

I'll probably manage to forgive myself for all of it; but slowly, for the rest of my life.

I walked on, my own demons needing to be quenched.

'Coffee?'

'Leave off, Charlie,' I said, fixing myself a fresh smoke and taking several heavy puffs. 'I didn't make time to drink breakfast and I'm straight-up thirsty. You know the drill: a bottle – imported – and a shot – raw.'

He didn't move.

'Did I stutter?'

'A little early, even for you, no?'

'It's noon somewhere,' I shot back, 'and, best I figure, you're not my mother and you're not my priest.'

Neutral silence. I lit a second cigarette off the first, the corrugated veins of my bleached-clean hands pulsing for no reason and without rhyme, and went right on regarding him through the haze until he turned round.

'You hear?' he asked over his shoulder, getting the order.

'No, what?'

'There's a girl missing,' he said, putting the drinks down in front of me. 'A local kid. The mother says she ain't been seen since the day before yesterday.'

'Huh.'

'It's been all over the news since two nights ago. What sort of private dick are you, you don't know this?'

'The idle sort.' I pushed the shot down and started in on the beer, not for the first time or the hundredth. 'And another thing: everywhere, even somewhere as small and crummy as this, needs to have at least one guy who provides the kind of service I do. So I hung out my shingle, because nobody else was fixing to hang out theirs.'

A few more large pulls, then I asked, 'They say how old?'

A blank stare.

'The girl,' I prompted, already swallowing the dregs.

'Fifteen, I think.'

'Fifteen forever,' I mumbled.

'What's that?'

'Nothin'. Listen, set me up with the same again, will you? This thirst is worse than I thought.'

'Sure thing,' he said, turning back to the bottles as I reached for my thinning leather poke.

It was then I heard the door open and close somewhere behind me; felt someone familiar settle in beside me. He'd aged badly the last time I saw him, now he was well on his way to just being old. His mouth was speared with an unlit cigarette and he looked like he was dressed in memory of a bad joke or in honour of a lost bet. Lots of people over the years had found out too late it was easy to underestimate him.

'Hello again, Shingfield,' I muttered without lifting my head.

'You look rough as usual,' was how he started, his fat voice coming out in a slow wheeze, as if the effort of communicating this way was asking too much of him. 'Do I need to ask how you're taking your whisky these days?'

'Any way I can get it, especially if I can get it straight up. As a matter of fact, I put a huge dent in the Highland Park last night then threw up on the wrong side of the toilet bowl. When I woke up this morning, the room smelled of booze and fear.'

'How'd she like that?'

'I'm sure she didn't like it much but I wasn't paying for feedback.'

'Damn, did you ever meet a drink you didn't like the taste of or a woman you didn't like the look of?'

'Nope, but I once saw a polar bear at the zoo.'

'Jesus.'

'Who he?'

'For Christ's sake. Always the same old shit with you.' He sighed. 'I must need my fucking head read coming to you on something like this.' He closed his eyes tight for several seconds. 'Let me have a pint, barman. Something local. And charge it up with my friend's here. His full tab, and whatever he's thirsty for after.'

'You don't need to do that,' I protested, although we all knew my heart wasn't in it.

'I know,' he said, 'I want to.'

15

'Much obliged,' I said, wiping my lips with the palm of my right hand. 'What'll it cost me?'

'We've got real talk to do.'

'Okay, I'm listening. What is it?'

'Maybe I could use your help on somethin'.'

'Uh huh.'

'You know about the kid?'

'Of course. I was just telling Charlie here all about it,' I said, nodding my head at Charlie as he put three fresh ones on the bar. 'What's the latest?'

'Her name's Emily Clark. You know the family?'

'Probably by sight at least. You?'

'Sure. Town this size, doing what I do, gets so I know everybody and, sooner or later, everybody knows me. Anyway, the kid lives over in the flats with her mother and her mother's latest boyfriend. Born without consent into a shitty world; an only child that never did nothin' to nobody and who in all likelihood won't see sixteen 'cause the woman who should care more about her than anybody else is a junky who can scarcely remember the last time she set eyes on the fruit of her womb.'

'And?'

'And nothin'. There's no foolin' here. I'm givin' it to you straight-up 'cause the magic forty-eight hours are over and I can't get a corner on it. We're hurtin' for information on this one. I'm workin' harder than a big girl's bra but gone are the minutes when my phone was blowin' up like a Baghdad market.'

'How'd you like the boyfriend?' I asked.

'I liked him a whole lot. Right until I found out he's spent the last five days locked up on a drink-driving charge. He's still there now 'cause what he did was a parole violation.'

'That's too bad.'

16

'Too bad is right. It never falls so easy.'

A pause as we each took a hit of our drinks. The only thing careful about his physical appearance, I was reminded as the glass parted his lips, were his teeth: so white, so straight, that they couldn't possibly have started out in his mouth.

'And the mother's definitely a no-go?' I asked.

'Definitely. She may be an addict, which is what she is, but that's all she is. We canvassed the whole area, spoke with the family and friends and neighbours and people she used to work with back when she could hold down a job, and they all, to a man and woman, said she loves that kid with all her heart. I've been here before, sadly, many times, and I know the differences between how innocent people act and how guilty people think they should act. Her pain is real. You ask me, I'll tell you she's not got a thing to do with it.'

'Give it to me as a percentage,' I said.

'One hundred per cent the mother's not involved,' he said with no hesitation. 'I seen her. I know. Trust me.'

'I do,' I said, also with no hesitation. 'Witnesses?'

'None.'

'Sightings?'

'Zilch.'

'Leads?'

'Nada.'

'That don't leave too much.' I reached for one of my drinks.

'No, it don't,' Shingfield said, reaching for his.

We each took another long swallow.

'Junk, you said?' I asked.

'The mother, yes. Isn't it always?' Shingfield said.

'Perhaps. Or maybe it just seems that way, especially to me. Where does the mother score?'

17

'We don't know for certain.'

'But we both know who it has to be, somewhere along the line.'

'Like I said, we don't know for sure.'

'Okay, how about this way: any suspects that weren't locked up at the time of the girl's disappearance?'

'None that are any good.'

'Did you check him out?'

'Who?'

'Stop with the fucking strigiform impersonation. You fucking know who.'

'Robinson?'

'Absolutely.'

'His alibi won't budge.'

'It never does.'

'I don't have enough to get a warrant.'

'A warrant? What's that?'

'I thought as much. Which is exactly why I'm here.'

I nodded that I understood.

'But remember this, Carmichael,' he went on, 'it might not be him. This isn't a big place but, believe it or not, there are other people who break the law.'

'If you say so, officer.'

'The fuck does that mean?'

'It means I was born at night but it wasn't last night.'

'Let's get back to the girl,' Shingfield continued, making no attempt to keep the urgency out of his voice.

'Shoot.'

'She was last seen by her mother sittin' on top of her bed. We checked. Twice. She ain't on top of it no more.'

'Going on three days,' I said, thinking out loud.

'Don't say it, okay. Just say you'll do what you can and you won't forget to call me when – *if* – you have somethin'.'

18

'I will do. And I won't forget.'

'Good. And, that being the case, don't forget this, either: you get caught pokin' around somewhere without probable or paperwork, I don't know you and I won't wanna know you. Understood?'

Another nod.

'Be in touch,' he said.

'Soon as I know something.'

He finished his drink in one long swallow, slid off the stool and went back out the way he'd come in.

It was only after he'd gone I noticed the photograph he'd left on the bar, probably given to him by the mother or maybe a neighbour. It was a grainy image of a girl who could pass for sixteen or twenty-six, depending on accessories and environment. I stared at it for a long time, then put it in the inside pocket of my jacket.

I could feel a hint of anger starting to get born at the back of my skull.

Here we go again, I thought.

'Another round, Charlie. Looks like tomorrow's gonna be a long one.'

I drowned the remains of the day in drink, at the cop's expense, and went home to bed. My sleep was dark and fitful and filled with dreams of missing children.

I woke up in the shivering dawn, opened my eyes most of the way, and lit a cigarette. I could hear rain but looked out the window and there wasn't any. There were no other sounds except for the building's settling groans.

I had a wet shit and a dry shave and went back out into the world. The mortuary lab I soon found myself in was a functional space fit for one very specific purpose. I figured it as the best place to start.

The pathologist in charge of post-mortem analysis,

who'd helped me bury more than bodies over the years, was redolent of death, though probably he no longer noticed it. His eyes, pale and glassy, were the colour of boiled milk.

'She ain't here, Carmichael,' he said. 'I've had only two fresh stiffs come in in the past seventy-two hours and ain't none of them a teenage girl.'

'If she is dead, she'd have had to come through you or the fellas upstairs?'

'Absolutely. We're the only game in town.'

'I appreciate you letting me tick the box.'

I was soon on my way to more familiar ground, eager to wash the mealy taste of death from my mouth.

'Don't you know the taste of water, Carmichael?' he persisted.

'I only drink it when I'm wet,' I said, fixing him with a stare that could stop a clock. 'Besides, this here's a bar, last time I looked. And you're the fucking bartender, are you not?'

'Bar owner.'

'Excuse me?'

'This is my bar. I'm the owner.'

'But you're Charlie. And there's a sign outside says this is Rae's.'

'Rae was the guy who sold it to me.'

'I stand corrected, boss.' I wondered how a man whose every gesture reeked of prison, despite efforts at concealment, had managed to get hold of the necessary loans and licences, but said nothing about it. 'Now, how about them drinks.'

'It's your liver. What'll you have?'

'Fucking Christ. One of each. Always one of each.'

Neither of my hands started reaching for either of my pockets.

'Who's paying?' he asked.

'The cop.'

'The cop ain't here no more.'

'But you know he's good for it.'

'No, I don't know that.'

'Sure you do. You also know that my face don't fit in any other bar within a ten-mile radius, which is one of the many reasons I'm in here more days than not. You'll get paid. Just set up the fucking drinks.'

Which he did, to his credit. The shot was history and the bottle was on its heels before either of us said another word. When it came, it was his, 'How's that thing coming along?'

'What thing's that?'

'The thing. The girl.'

'Oh, that. I tried the death house. The angle was empty.'

'That's too bad.'

'Too bad she ain't dead?'

'You know what I mean.'

'I do. I can live with too bad. I can't live with too late. Let me have another round, then I'll be on my way.'

He did, and I was.

'I heard you gave one of my girls a mouthful.'

'Isn't that the whole point?'

'I'm serious here.'

'What girl?'

'At the motel.'

'What motel? What's this about?'

'She said you gave her a load of shit about a twenty-pound note. Made her feel small.'

'Ah, her,' I said, making a deprecatory gesture with both hands, which encouraged a column of smoke from the cigarette in my right to climb up toward the ceiling. 'A real cold fish, that one. It's like this: I don't pay your girls to nag. I want that, I'll get me a wife. Tell your friend to toughen up. If she can't, she's in the wrong game. And while you're at it, tell her to stop treating her ass like it's the last of the world's wonders.'

'I'll pass on your pearls.'

'Look, I don't have time for this. You know what I'm here looking for. Can you help me or can't you?'

'Nothing's that easy.'

'I know, I know. Everybody needs to eat. Listen, you give me a start on this thing, I'll make sure you're taken care of. You have my word.'

'What's that worth?'

'My word? Hell, it's all I have. That means it's worth a lot.'

The only noise for a few seconds was the ticking of a clock.

I realised I was holding my breath as she added it all up.

'Okay,' she said at last, 'here it is: I heard there might be some military involvement.'

That I wasn't expecting. It seemed as if there was enough in it already without the army. 'The fuck you talking about?'

'Just what I said. I heard it was a soldier boy killed her.'

'She might not be dead.'

'Good one.'

I knew she was right. Nobody was looking for a girl. Everybody was looking for a corpse.

'Is there a name?' I asked.

'There usually is.'

'Well, hit me with it.'

'Just like that?'

'Sure. Didn't we do this bit already?'

'We did, and I'll hold you to more later, but I'm hungry now.'

'For fuck sake. I've met starving piranhas with less bite than your lot.'

I fished out my last note, silently thanking Shingfield for the tab and for putting the extras in the wood. 'You got change for a twenty?'

'Nope, and I don't want to hear no pat-me-on-the-head lecture about Scottish pioneers, either,' she said, snapping the money and pocketing it. 'The name I heard was Major Boniness. B-O-N-I-N-E-S-S.'

'Major? This smells like bullshit, lady.'

'Maybe, but that's all I got. Take it or leave it.'

'You're pushing your luck, dick.'

'I know that much, Charlie, and I'm sure it must be hard for you to watch, but with me, thirst always trumps pride.'

'Play that music someplace else, pal. This here's a business.'

'I know that, but I'm already half in the bag so all's it'll take is a couple of rounds to get me straight, then I'll be out of your hair.'

'I've got mouths at home, same as the next guy.'

'I know that, too, and if we can agree on one more round of the usual, I swear to Jesus Christ on the fucking cross you won't see my face again until the lawman's cleared the slate.'

'Either I get paid or I don't see you no more. Is that what I'm hearing?'

'Exactly.'

He mulled it over for a full minute. Lots of big thinkers in this city.

'Then it's your basic win-win,' he said, pouring the shot then reaching for the fridge. The bottle frothed a little after he'd put it down, spilling some beer onto the bar.

'So,' he continued, watching me drink, 'any luck yet?'

'None at all.' A pause. 'Well, I got a bite but it don't mean nothing to me.'

'Care to share?'

My turn to mull.

'As long as it goes no further,' I said.

'Who'd I tell, even if I wanted to?'

I hesitated again, then, 'My source says it's likely a soldier took the girl. Could be hc told a hooker he has her and nobody picked up on it, including me.

'Military, huh?'

'A Major. Goes by the name of Boniness.'

'What?' he asked, his back to me again as he dug a washcloth out of a bucket in the corner.

'Boniness.'

'How are you spelling that?'

'B-O-N-I-N-E-S-S.'

'Wait,' he said, facing me now but distracted from wiping the bar. 'Give me that again.'

'Christ. Let me have a pencil.'

He did.

I wrote the whole thing – Major Boniness – as best I could on a damp napkin and turned it around so he could read it.

He stared at it for a very long time. Finally he said, 'Holy fucking shit. You cracked it, Carmichael, and you didn't even realise it.'

'What the fuck is this? What are you saying?'

'The name of the bastard who did it. It's right here.'

'Where?'

'Here,' he said, pointing a gnarled index at the napkin. 'Look. I'll show you.'

I did look and he did show me. And I saw it. The truth that had been staring me in the face from the very start.

'Charlie, my boy, you're a genius,' I said, pleased, but embarrassed, too, because I've been long enough in this game and should have seen it. Maybe this particular bar owner was right; maybe my head was getting too wet for this work.

I was off the stool and out the door as he shouted at my back, 'Wait. You've left half your beer.'

The KoKo Kavern was bursting at the seams with men willing to hand over the housekeeping for over-priced drink and three-minute dances with pouting jailbait. It was the last place left to look because I now knew it was where I'd find her; where I always knew she'd be. With him.

Him. James Robinson. You name it, he makes money from it. Amazingly, he manages to do it all without hardly showing himself. Most people know the name, precious few civilians have seen the adult face. Many of them that have seen it can't paint you a picture of it. It's impossible to paint when you're sleeping under six feet of cement.

I'm an exception to the rule because I've seen his face and I'm still breathing. He looks close enough to being like a normal man but there's a hole inside him where emotion is supposed to be.

I cut a path through the crowd, toward the far end of the place, and was still about ten metres away from where I wanted to be when I spotted the gym monkey on guard duty in front of the back office.

The monkey's eyes were fixed on the tight arse of a young piece of stage tail so he didn't see me coming until it was too late. He opened his mouth then, creating an exit, but nothing came out. I gave him one in the teeth, hard, and that closed the shop.

He folded like a lazy geriatric after the second tap, falling over forward and landing on what was left of his face. He'd wake up with a headache a mile long, but knowing he woke up only because I'd allowed it.

The door was closed but not locked. I didn't knock.

The hooker from the motel was spot on. Robinson is small in the same way they say Texas is small. He got up from behind his desk when he saw me come in; his enormous frame, which rose in stages, shielding the rear exit I knew was there. There were bales of banded notes spilling out of the open safe to his right. He hadn't been expecting unpaid company.

'Hello, Augie,' he said. 'Long time. This a pinch?'

He knows my first name because we were kids together in the old neighbourhood. He also knows I've got no love for either, the name or the neighbourhood. When we'd grown up a bit – no longer boys but not yet men – we played poker in back rooms after the real games had broken up and the players had gone home rich or rooked. He was horrendous at the felt and I cleaned him out of smokes and small coins more times than I can count.

But all of that was a long time ago. Before he became the faceless go-to-guy for a recreational high. And before the other thing: before Linda.

'I'd say hello,' I said, 'but don't know what to call you. Word on the street these days is you prefer a variation of your name as it appears on your driver's licence. Trust you to give yourself the top rank. And no, this isn't a pinch. You know I don't do that no more.'

'Can't.'

'How's that?'

'Can't. You *can't* do it no more, even if you wanted to. No authority, right?'

'That's right. In the legal sense, at least.'

He looked at me, his stare cutting like a bone-saw. He was measuring me for a coffin. I threw it right back at him the best I could, my eyes burning with animal hatred.

'Won't you sit?' he asked.

26

'I can talk on my feet.'

'Do you know you're a pain in the neck?'

'I could have guessed it.'

'Nuts to you. Listen, where's my guy at?' he asked in the gravel voice that always gave me a feeling like an injection of ice water in the spine.

'Him? He's taking a little nap.'

'You just can't get no quality staff these days.'

'Is that so?'

'If I say it is, yeah. You wearing any iron?'

'Not me, Jimmy. I'm just a regular citizen.'

'Whatever you say,' he said, flashing me his heater.

'It doesn't have to go down this way.'

'Sure it does, so let me tell you again: you don't want this,' he smiled. 'We're in different divisions.'

I remembered what he never knew: that in life, as in poker, you play the man, not the hand or situation. And as big as Robinson was, he was slow. A fearsome reputation's not worth shit when your protection guy has been laid low and you're no longer fast enough to look after yourself.

He saw the blackjack but not soon enough. His smile went sideways when I sapped him a good one on the temple. I never in my life hit anything harder. He was unconscious before his body landed awkwardly on the floor, his right foot at an unnatural angle to his right leg. There would be conscious pain, too, but that would come later, after I'd taken a powder. For the moment, I knew from the way I'd hit him and the way he'd fallen that he wouldn't be awake again for a while.

I found Emily in the back room. She looked almost exactly the same as she had the last time I'd looked at the photograph, except this time she was dead. The blameless skin of her naked corpse – skin so pale a white heat would have set it on fire – was covered with bruises. For a brief moment I felt like I was going to shoot my cookies again, so I closed my eyes and gritted my teeth. And it passed, as it almost always does.

I picked up the phone – 'Detective Shingfield, please. No, I don't care to give my name' – then, having used my handkerchief to wipe off everything I'd touched and being careful to avoid even looking at the money, stepped round Robinson's prostrate mass, with no intention of going out the way I'd come in.

My stool was waiting.

Money

after George V. Higgins' *The Friends of Eddie Coyle*

When Maurice Abrahams came downstairs the morning it happened, his wife wasn't making bacon and eggs and there was no coffee ready because of the two men wearing balaclavas and holding pistols.

'We know who you are, Mr Abrahams,' the man to his wife's right said. Maurice Abrahams estimated him to be at least six five. 'We know you're today's duty manager at the Savings and Loans National on Stovington Boulevard. That should tell you something right off. Me and you, we're going down to the bank while my friend waits here with your wife. She'll be fine, released unharmed, if you do what I tell you to do when I tell you to do it. So will you. Be fine. If you don't do what you're told when you're told, if you deviate in even one small way, both of you will get shot. Your wife first. Now, say something to let me know you understand.'

'I'll do whatever you say. Just don't hurt her, okay?' Maurice Abrahams said through clenched teeth, hands balled into impotent fists at his sides.

'That's up to you,' Mr Tall said. 'Put on your coat and pick up your briefcase.'

Maurice Abrahams, at fifty, prided himself on being fit and healthy, physically strong. He held a position of considerable responsibility at a respectable firm and was tipped to go even further. In short, he was a successful man, unaccustomed to being told what to do. But he put on his coat and picked up his briefcase, then turned to his wife. 'Try not to be frightened, dear. Everything will work out. I promise.'

'Your husband's right,' Mr Tall said. 'We're not here

29

to hurt you. We get the money and nobody does nothing stupid, then nobody gets hurt.' He took Maurice Abrahams by the elbow and ushered him toward the back door. 'Time to go to work, Mr Abrahams.'

On a street next to the house there was a black Honda Civic. A third man, also wearing a balaclava, sat in the driver's seat. He said nothing when Maurice Abrahams got in the back seat with Mr Tall.

Mr Honda started the engine, indicated, and pulled away from the kerb.

They sat in silence for a couple of short blocks, then Mr Tall said, 'No doubt your mind's racing all over the place. Us. Your wife. What'll happen when we get to the bank. And you're maybe thinking about being a hero. I'm telling you now: don't. Just don't do it. All we want's the money. We don't want nobody hurt. Keep calm and be smart. Think of that pretty little wife of yours. You going to be smart, Mr Abrahams?'

Maurice Abrahams *was* smart. People had always told him this. And silent co-operation seemed to be the smart move here. In point of fact, sitting in a strange car, armed with only a briefcase and staring down the barrels of a pair of what he had to assume were loaded guns, it was the *only* move.

He nodded his head.

'That's real good,' Mr Tall said. 'What I want you to do now is crouch down in the foot well so you can't see nothing.'

Again, Maurice Abrahams did as he'd been told.

'Now close your eyes tight,' Mr Tall said. 'I'm taking my mask off and so is the driver, until we get there.'

Maurice Abrahams closed his eyes. He wanted to get a look at the men but didn't want his wife to get hurt, or worse. He tried not to berate himself for being so easily compliant. No doubt there would be plenty of time afterwards for self-recrimination.

'Right, listen to hear, Mr Abrahams,' Mr Tall said, interrupting what was already a very fragmented jumble of thoughts, 'because this is important. When we arrive at the bank, we'll go in the employees' entrance. Same as you did yesterday and the day before. Same as you always do. When we're in, tell your staff to keep the doors locked. Tell them nobody calls the police or pushes the silent alarm, otherwise they'll get hurt. And so will your wife. I know when the time lock opens. We'll wait for that. I'll take out the money, then you and me, we'll get back in the car and my friend here will drive us away. Before we leave the bank, you tell your staff again not to do nothing stupid after we're gone or people will end up getting shot. They aren't to contact the authorities until they hear back from you. Do you understand?'

Maurice Abrahams said nothing. He nodded again.

'Don't forget through any of this that I have a gun. And the man at your house, where your wife is, he's got a gun, too.'

'Everything is clear,' Maurice Abrahams said. 'I won't give you any trouble.'

Most of the employees just stood and listened, slack-jawed and ashen-faced, as Maurice Abrahams explained the situation. A couple of the women cried quietly.

'The vault will open soon,' Mr Tall said. 'I'll get what it is I came for and then I'll be on my way with Mr Abrahams. You're not to do nothing until you hear from him. We have his wife. Any of you colour outside the lines here, she'll be dead and her death will be on your hands. Remember that.'

At the exact time the vault made a soft clicking sound, Mr Tall instructed Maurice Abrahams to put in the code and turn the handle. He did so, steadying his hands as best he could in case they suspected him of stalling, then moved out of the way.

Mr Tall, *his* hands steady, took four large plastic bags out of his coat. He filled each of them to the top with used notes of all denominations.

When Mr Tall had finished, he told Maurice Abrahams to close and lock the vault. Maurice Abrahams did so.

Mr Tall spoke to the bank employees again, one final reminder, then he and Maurice Abrahams left by the door they'd come in through, each of them carrying two of the bags.

Maurice Abrahams was back in the foot well, eyes closed, as the Civic drove for what seemed like a half hour but was likely only ten or fifteen minutes.

Finally, the car stopped. A door opened.

'You can open your eyes, Mr Abrahams,' Mr Tall said, 'and get up out of there.'

Maurice Abrahams opened his eyes. Mr Tall and Mr Honda had put their balaclavas back on. A cold sweat broke out on Maurice Abrahams' forehead when he looked out the window, not at his house, the home where his wife was being held hostage by an armed criminal, but at a large expanse of green grass he didn't recognise.

'You've been very helpful, Mr Abrahams. Thanks for playing the smart hand,' Mr Tall said.

'What's this? Where are we?' Maurice Abrahams asked. 'What am I supposed to do now?'

'You get out and start walking.'

Maurice Abrahams did exactly that, not daring to run until the car, with Mr Honda behind the wheel and Mr Tall still in the back, now with room enough to count his money, had turned a corner and was out of sight.

Fruit of Thy Womb

I can't say I meant it and I can't say I didn't mean it. It just sort of, happened. Alone with it indoors – we lived in a block of flats that was tall with broad shoulders, where hundreds and maybe thousands of strangers endured in rented spaces, all squashed in and floating around like dry fish – I couldn't understand why there was still so much noise. I'd fed it, washed and clothed it, held it an inch from my breast until I felt sure it was asleep. But as soon as I put it down it would start bawling again. True to say I lost all sense of the world beyond the walls; lost all expectation of an end to such an assault on my senses.

As the sound became too much, penetrating my core, it was no longer in my arms. I watched, wordless – watched its searching eyes, its open mouth, its red skin – until all of it, its whole body, was on the floor.

My only child. His father's son. The boy about whom strangers would stop me in the street to confirm he must surely be the apple of my eye.

But they didn't see the worms that plagued me: the rotten isolation of this kind of life, the untimely dreams gone forever; the hollow, often-absent tree this clamorous seed had fallen unbidden from. They didn't see none of that, because nobody does. Nobody wants to.

His little clothes and the carpet, worn in places from all the pacing, muffled somewhat the noise of impact, which sounded to me like a bone breaking underwater.

The crying worsened then, probably from the pain, and didn't stop – *really* stop – until, bending down over his husk, I put the palm of my right hand over the red mouth, my fingers digging into the bruised cheeks.

Peace at last.

Although, as dawn broke cold the following morning and I realised what had been done, the rational pieces of my mind weren't so easy to reclaim.

Marion Morrison Stole My Hat

I rose to my feet under a burnt-yellow sky and discarded the half-drunk almond-scented coffee that, only moments before, had held my attention. I'd been distracted by the sight of the figure from my waking dreams. So distracted, in fact, I neglected to pick up my hat from the table that was home to the cup I no longer cared about.

It was a little before ten in the morning, the temperature lower than expected for the time of year. If the cold snap continued, I'd likely need the hat; but all such thoughts seemed to have vanished, like mist in a rainstorm.

He was standing by the side of the road, broad shoulders levelled out above his protruding chest. That chin – so solid, so reassuring – was out, too, as if to warn against an assault from the so-called Indians of another era's moving pictures.

I tried to make eye contact with him, but couldn't. I even called out his stage name – 'John! John!' – but didn't make a dent, the words seemingly getting lost in the forever distance between us.

Suddenly he was gone, enveloped by the crowd. My legs carried me backward and forward as I looked in every direction, peered in every corner; the panic and sense of loss no less real for the situation's lack of genuine import.

Then, turning back in the direction I had come, I saw it: my hat. Unmistakable, really, that pinch-front, triangle-crease in silverbelly with snakeskin band and diamondback rattler. It was moving above a sea of oblivious heads, away from me, framing, although I couldn't see them from where I was, the cobalt-blue eyes of a native Iowan who stood over six feet tall.

The one-time all-American hero whose daylight treachery broke my heart.

Nothing More Than a Whisper

after Salman Rushdie's *In the South*

It happened in early summer as rays from the fledgling sun poked through misty clouds and fell, dappled, onto the streets below. No-one was surprised when he fell, nor were they surprised that his body – once so strong, so reassuring in its blatant masculinity, but then very frail, a shade among shadows – made what some people heard as only a token noise on impact. More vital were the surrounding sounds of singing birds and blaring speakers; of women and their children, who shrieked with a mixture of fear and delight as they skipped between the bumpers of too-close taxis in pursuit of rainbow puddles. All of it the soundtrack to the final moments in Victor's life.

He'd been sitting at an interior booth, *their* booth, of the café where he'd gone near daily during the preceding five years, sipping coffee from a small porcelain cup. Strong and black; the way, he was fond of saying, he'd liked his women, when he'd still had an inkling for that part of life. With him in the booth was Alex, the only person left in the world, it seemed, who knew him.

'Today you don't seem so good,' Alex said, not looking at his friend but at the large mug of milky tea he was lowering from his lips. 'Yesterday, too.'

'I'm fine,' Victor said, raising his eyes to look, in turn, at what he saw as the pale face of a man whose name he sometimes forgot. 'Except that I can't sleep. Not anymore.'

'How long has it been?'

'Since what? Since I last slept?'

'Sure.'

'At least several days, I think. Who can tell?'

'What do you do instead?'

'Instead of sleeping, you mean?'

'Yes.'

'From time to time I'll sit on top of the bed and read a newspaper, but my eyes aren't what they used to be. Mostly I lie there in the inky blackness and stare at the damp spot on the ceiling until either I fall asleep or it's a reasonable time to get up and face the day.'

Victor ought to have been tired enough to sleep well and long. He'd married young and his wife, who was some kind of Irish, and fertile, had given him two girls and a boy before the rings had been on their fingers five years. This, coupled with a demanding career as a mid-level civil servant, meant he had little time for leisure, such as the sports, badminton chief among them, that had so consumed him in his boyhood.

With retirement came more opportunities, but by then he was reduced to occasional moments alone at the desk in his study; and, if he was lucky, the book in his hands was sufficiently engaging for him to want to spend several consecutive hours with it.

Before long his wife was dead and the children he loved, and, he knew, who loved him, had moved away to pursue ideas of their own. Alone for the first time in his adult life, and lonely with it, mortality was undeniably closer than ever. It cast a dark shadow across each of his days, one often indistinguishable from the other.

It was perhaps this inevitability, suddenly so immediate, so very real, that caused him to take stock. He soon concluded that his had been a disappointing existence; one where the sum total of successes sought and earned may have outweighed the losses, but not by much. It was the sheer ordinariness of it all that struck him most keenly. A marriage. Children. A job. The inescapable truth was he'd turned out to be merely average, with nothing to distinguish him from all of the other men and women he'd come in contact with over the decades. He was certainly no more special than even the lowest among them.

This was all inner turmoil, of course. Only rarely did he allow the disappointment of his calculation to outwardly manifest itself. He hailed from traditional stock; from a generation of menfolk that valued stoicism above all else. The mistakes made and opportunities missed gave birth to his personal beast of burden. Never, he vowed, would he allow such things to become someone else's concern.

In these latter years, it was only with Alex that he felt in any sense alive, for it was in his company that he could, within his own agreed limits, voice some of the things that were troubling him. More than that, and ashamedly so, he took comfort in hearing that Alex, likewise, did not have his problems to seek.

What neither man could see was that they were, and had been, each of them comparatively fortunate, having lived long lives in comfort in the company of family members who loved them, among other reasons, for their predictable dependability. It was primarily this characteristic that defined them.

These traits were also evident in their shared routine, one element of which was the Thursday trip to the post office to collect their pensions. Victor didn't go for the money necessarily; he had enough of that to pay the bills, with a little left over to pay for small luxuries from time to time, such as a hot drink when out with his friend.

In fact, it was there, outside the post office, that Victor fell. With the weekly cheque in his jacket pocket – a cheque he would never cash – and Alex walking along beside him, Victor pushed though the heavy front doors to get back out onto the street. The last thing he would have seen while still vertical was the sunlit path whose uneven surface may or may not have caused the fall. The noise of afternoon traffic on the adjacent street contributed to the muffling of both his groan and the sound his bones made when they landed, weakened but heavy, on the grass of the post-office lawn that ran parallel to the path.

'Please,' Alex said to the paramedic in the back of the ambulance, 'we are each other's only pal. I've never once considered how it would be without him – without anyone – in what are surely the last years of my life. Honestly,' he continued, oblivious to the paramedic's unconvincing statements that his friend was likely to be fine, 'I always thought I'd go before him.'

The world kept turning that day, and has been turning thus from that day to this, yet Alex's small part of it was irrevocably changed. Notably, during the few short months that he endured before joining Victor in the ground, he never again sat in their booth, nor did he collect any more pension cheques.

'What's the point?' no-one heard him ask aloud.

What Goes Around

Seven. I skirt the lake's perimeter under cover of a plunging darkness that is broken only by the dim light of a waxing crescent moon. The noise of my footsteps edging through the thick brush disturbs the silence in a way that the muffled shot of only moments ago did not.

Six. With practised ease, I disassemble the component parts of the bolt-action rifle I'd purchased, using an alias, and modified to suit my own, specific purpose. Butt. Stock. Trigger guard. Trigger. Bolt handle. Bolt. Forestock. Chamber. Barrel. Sight. Muzzle. Each element lands in the water and sinks without trace to the bottom. The relief at having disposed of it is immediate, profound.

Five. I watch his involuntary reactions to the impact of the nickel-tipped mercury bullet, knowing that, inside, the liquid, having punctured the plug, would be cutting its way through flesh and bone, tissue and gristle, annihilating the cranial cavity. Crude but effective. Fatality guaranteed. I can't see the plate-sized exit wound from where I am, but I know it's there. The last thing I do see before getting up and away is the obliteration of his upper mandible. I feel neither sadness nor excitement. As he said, I feel nothing at all.

Four. I slide back the bolt, put a shell into the breech, push the bolt forward, and look down the telescopic sight, getting my eye in. Seeing him this way, I am surprised to feel an electric flash of desire in the pit of my stomach, a familiar warmth between my thighs. Such thoughts are quickly cast aside: my mind is settled. The anticipatory odour of death fills my nostrils. I take a deep breath in, out. Again. My actions are now slow, deliberate, *necessary*, as I alter my position, hold my arms and hands steady, take aim, and squeeze the trigger.

Three. The *why* – this time only, a combination of

professional and personal – was clear. The *how*, *where* and *when* were decided after many weeks of meticulous consideration. Nothing would be left to chance. It can be no other way, of course. My survival in this business – and it is my survival, not the business itself, that I value above all else – depends on such relentless attention to detail.

Two. When my handler showed me the mark, I couldn't believe it was really him. Him. The man who took my heart, then broke it. I was to be paid for something I'd fantasised about for years; something I'd do for no charge.

One. 'I don't want to do this any longer,' he said. A sudden downpour, curt but insistent, did not break the flow of his words; a hand across the hair falling down across his forehead the only indication he was aware of the rain. His voice was strong, the words certain, likely rehearsed, 'The secrets, the lies, the last-minutes changes of plan. The no-shows. It's over.'

Where Crocodiles Sleep

I'm not much more than a lush and a coward but there's something about children that stirs my blood no end. Their slender waists and flat tummies, their blameless skin. The innocent protuberance of a schoolgirl's hairless pubic bone. The milky sweetness of a teenage boy's first ejaculation.

I had one in the garage with me then, some kid from the neighbourhood. Brian, I think. I'd snatched him up from under a bruised purple sky as the Sun was getting ready to die for the day.

I could sense ghosts hovering in the air around us, between the dust motes and the oil smell, as I leaned in to do it. The metal of his wheelchair was cold against my bare shins, the weight of it heavy like an iron lung, and I knew that somewhere demons would be hauling themselves out of fiery pits as we – Brian and me – crossed that line together, sharing something that could never be forgotten. The incarnadine tears he cried told me he knew it, too.

The noise from the spastic fury of Brian's thrashing limbs must have guided them because soon there were voices.

'I think he took him in there. Listen. Can you hear that? Brian?'

I coughed my involuntary post-ejaculation cough and dead butterflies fell out of my mouth.

'Open the door, you fucking monster, and let the boy go.'

They knew me for what I am, of course. The authorities had informed them of the breed of my particular beast just prior to my descent into their hubristic world and, in spite of their best efforts, I soon had a new lair. The school, it seemed, just happened to be nearby.

More voices. Louder now. Urgent. Frenzied. And banging. Lots of banging. The door almost off its hinges.

It won't be long, Brian, I promise. Soon I'll have to face the wrath of rebel angels, then we can all go back to how it was before. The only thing different will be the sky. I wonder how long I'll have to wait to see it again, and what colour it will be.

A Short Story of Murder

Ailshem is more than twenty miles from the nearest town. Its inhabitants' rough, nasal accent is often difficult for outsiders to interpret. The landscape that sits below semi-permanent grey skies is strikingly flat and offers remarkable views of endless fields with almost unlimited hues of green. The few tall buildings are easily visible long before the small town's outer limits have been reached. There isn't much else to see. Even the solitary motel, arguably the most impressive structure, is rarely noticed by those who pass through. A small café sits next door. It is owned by a dour woman who never smiles as she serves coffee and homemade cakes in winter and cold drinks and ice-creams in summer. There is also a post office, a bank, a grocer's and a hardware shop. The people of Ailshem, although tight-lipped and stoic, are nonetheless content and, for the most part, prosperous. They add to the community's overall solidity. Ailshem people are dependable.

Their idyllic calm was permanently shattered one morning near to the end of December 1978 by the unmistakable sound of gunshots. With it, the serenity that Ailshem's residents had cultivated and protected was destroyed; the town's anonymity gone forever as, suddenly, stories of its violence were broadcast around the world. As three of their own lay dead, innocence and tranquillity were quickly replaced with suspicion and fear.

Ailshem's most prominent resident, retired school master Mr Harold Preece, was fifty-seven years old. In spite of his age, Mr Preece was a striking man: his height, broad shoulders, ruddy face and piercing eyes made sure of an impression. He had taught at the local high school for more

44

than three decades, including almost eighteen years as its no-nonsense principal, before taking early retirement, and therefore had an unrivalled familiarity with Ailshem's people. Mr Preece was also the Chairman of the Ailshem Residents' Association Committee, having stood unopposed for more years than anyone could remember, as well as an active organiser of the town's numerous social events.

Mr Preece had led a happy and successful life. His marriage to childhood sweetheart Elizabeth had given him three children; a son and two daughters. The two eldest were frequent and willing visitors to Ailshem. The youngest child, Annie, at only seventeen, still lived at home with her parents; attending the same school where her father had spent his entire career. Mr Preece's only cause for concern was his wife's deteriorating health. Although Mr Preece himself privately suspected mental-health issues, the doctors had so far offered no concrete diagnosis.

Mr Preece usually began his day just after seven o'clock in the morning by brewing a pot of strong coffee on the stove, then drinking one cup after the other while poring over a pile of newspapers. On that particular morning, however, he allowed himself to doze until it had gone almost nine. This was because Annie, celebrating her performance in the school's production of Shakespeare's *Macbeth* – she was roundly praised for her portrayal as wife to the Thane of Fife – had not returned home until late the night before. Mr Preece, although not concerned about his typically sensible daughter, couldn't break the habit of staying up and staying awake until she was safely home.

That night, as he heard his daughter's footsteps coming up the front walk, Mr Preece put his reading book on the side cabinet and rose from the familiar comfort of his well-worn green armchair. He peered out through the slats of the living-room window's blinds to see a young male sitting in the driver's seat of a sports car parked by the curb. Eddy Kasinski.

Eddy and Annie were classmates and had been dating for eighteen months. Eddy, whose lack of interest in his studies was widely known, had met with more than mild disapproval when he and Mr Preece had first met. Mr Preece's views had not softened and, although he had nothing against Eddy personally, made no secret of the fact he would prefer his daughter to keep company with someone more academically-minded.

Mr Preece spent more time seated at the kitchen table than in any other place in his home, except perhaps for his bedroom. The living room was warm and tastefully furnished but he preferred the ample space afforded him by the enormous oak table he had built shortly before the birth of his youngest child. He could spread the day's papers out across it and spend many undisturbed hours with them, often reading every article on every page. Mr Preece's appetite, once hearty and difficult to satisfy, had diminished significantly; to such an extent that he breakfasted only on fruit or a piece of toast. He had never smoked, not even pipes or cigars, and drank alcohol only when required by a social occasion.

After washing down a slightly bruised banana with cup after cup of black coffee, and after the varied content of that day's regional and national papers had been fully exhausted, Mr Preece, whose wife was still asleep upstairs, rinsed his cup in the sink and set it on the drainer. He sat back down to pull on his hiking boots.

Mr Preece breathed deeply, purposefully, as he crossed over the threshold, wrapped up tightly in coat, scarf, hat and gloves to protect against the frost so typical of the onset of winter. He savoured these brisk walks and never tired of treading the same route around the perimeter of his property.

That particular walk, on that particular day, would prove to be his last.

Although the owner, Margaret Proot, was almost permanently miserable and impolite, the café next to the motel was known for serving a decent menu at reasonable prices and therefore boasted a steady stream of local regulars.

The thirty-something man seated in a booth by the door was not a regular, however. Cyril South had a map on the table in front of him and was studying it carefully while sipping sugary white coffee and working his way through a pack of filter-tipped cigarettes. Cyril's outward calmness belied an inner apprehension. It was an important day; a dangerous day that potentially held substantial rewards. He was engrossed in the map because he intended to lie low, with a lot of time on the road, after the job was done. The towns circled on the map promised new adventures. More than that, they represented opportunities for a new start.

His worldly possessions were on the seat next to him: a battered black holdall with some old clothes, a couple of books, some more maps. The oily handgun hidden for the moment among a pair of rolled-up jeans was, he knew, a clear breach of his parole conditions.

After his third cup of coffee, Cyril glanced at the clock on the wall above the register before lifting his large, powerfully-built frame up from the seat. He put some crumpled notes on the table, no tip, hauled the bag over his shoulder, and headed for the door. Within a few minutes of stepping outside, a car pulled up to the kerb. The passenger-side door swung open even before it had come to a complete stop. Cyril placed the bag in the rear seat before sitting up front next to his friend, Dale.

Annie Preece, although not considered a traditional beauty, was certainly attractive. Tall, slim and active, with long brown hair framing a pretty face, she was well-liked by boys and girls and enjoyed the benefits of a wide social circle. In spite of this popularity, Eddy was her first and only boyfriend. Certainly, he was the only boy she had plucked up the courage required to introduce to her parents. He was not put off by their cool response, nor by the many probing questions asked of him by Annie's father.

Dressed only in a loose-fitting nightdress, eyes puffy with tiredness, Annie descended the stairs in her usual measured way to answer the telephone, unhurried by whoever was waiting on the line. She made her way into the kitchen, where she reached the house's only phone moments after it had stopped ringing.

Dale Townsend was driving an old black Ford. After Cyril had got in, Dale asked if he had remembered to bring the gun. Cyril assured him that he had.

'There's a kit in the boot, too,' Dale said.

Evidence produced at trial would show that this kit consisted of two sawn-off shotguns, ammunition, two pairs of gloves and a selection of carving knives.

Both men were wearing stained overalls and muddy boots. An early Rolling Stones song played on the radio as they drove along Ailshem's main street, Mick Jagger's searing vocals filling the car's small interior. Having served time together in a two-man cell, they were accustomed to each other's company and, as such, neither one of them felt the need to offer any small talk. They had been released within months of each other during the summer of the previous year. They reunited soon afterward, each toiling at a series of low-paid menial jobs while they plotted the particulars of this piece of work. As they saw it, having been deprived of their liberty for so long, of their God-given right to make a living, they were entitled now to make up for lost time by taking whatever they pleased away from people who had more than their share.

Although they had little in common besides a history of crime and time spent in various institutions, Cyril and twenty-seven-year-old Dale's friendship was nonetheless a solid one rarely marred by quarrels.

Dale's muscled physique projected a forceful presence that matched that of his burly former cellmate. Large areas of Dale's skin, including his hands and neck, were littered with the crude and amateurish markings of prison tattoos. A thick scar running down the left side of his face completed the look of a menacing individual who was surely no stranger to violence.

One other notable marking on Dale's skin was an angry red rash behind his right ear, caused by a dermatological condition that had plagued him since childhood. It wasn't painful but it itched terribly. Dale frequently clawed at it with his fingers and nails, looking to find some respite. It was an annoying habit that Cyril had no hesitation in rebuking him for.

Their first stop was at a nearby off-licence, where they bought eight bottles of cheap imported lager. Dale had almost finished one bottle even before he was back behind the wheel. Next, they went to a hardware shop where their only purchase was a length of rope. Afterwards, they sat in the car for a long time and drank some more.

They decided to have a late supper in one of Ailshem's two restaurants; a low-key diner that served unadventurous but tasty meals from early until late. They spent the absolute last of their money on large plates of sausages, mashed potatoes and mushrooms topped with generous helpings of homemade onion gravy. All of this was washed down with several bottles of beer.

Mr Harold Preece's wife, Kathryn, formerly Kathryn Peltzer, was the younger of two daughters born to wealthy landowners. She met Harold while they were in their final year of high school. Their courtship was brief and traditional and their love grew quickly. Richard, their first child, was born when the marriage was less than two years old and their elder daughter, Jane, was born when her brother, who shared many of his father's features, had just celebrated his third birthday. Mr and Mrs Preece were happy with their lot and were utterly surprised to learn the news of a third, unplanned pregnancy. At forty and thirty-nine, they had considered their family unit complete. That is not to say they were displeased. Mr Preece, in particular, was quietly thrilled at having another child; more precisely, a second daughter. The youngest of the Preece children would grow to be her father's favourite; a fact he made no effort to conceal.

Active in her youth and early adulthood, Mrs Preece was frustrated that her health had deteriorated since Annie was born. That is not to say that the pregnancy or the birth were to blame. They were not. As her body became less compliant, Mrs Preece spent an increasing amount of time in her bedroom with the door closed and the curtains drawn. The large wood-framed double bed and matching wardrobe in the room were purchased shortly after they had announced their engagement.

On the last day of her life, Kathryn Preece rose just before noon; almost three full hours after her husband had gone downstairs to read his newspapers and drink his coffee. This was not unusual. Mrs Preece was easily fatigued and would spend countless hours in bed; either reading second-hand paperback novels while lying atop the sheets or sleeping soundly beneath them.

After washing and dressing, she sat at her lacquered bureau and began completing the previous day's crossword in between a series of naps. At around seven in the evening, she went downstairs to prepare the family's dinner. In this manner, she passed what would be her final hours.

With headlights dimmed to such an extent that the glow they emitted was almost imperceptible, the Ford crept forward along the now-deserted streets of Ailshem. Cyril, with a map spread open on his lap, was giving Dale very precise directions as the car inched along in the gloom. It would not be long, he said, until they reached the house where the Preece family lived.

Annie Preece's bedroom was much smaller than that of her parents. Except for a few items of furniture – a single bed, a wardrobe with built-in drawers and a small writing desk – the room was uncluttered and considerably tidier than the bedrooms of other teenage girls. Even the books and revision notes on her desk were arranged in ordered piles. This neatness was undoubtedly something she had inherited from her father, who was known to be fastidious in everything he did; a trait that, as her own ability to manage the household diminished, quietly irked his wife.

Less than a week after the Preece family had eaten their final meal together, Eddy Kasinski, one of the last people to see Annie alive, was being interviewed under police caution at the police station in Marcombe; the nearest town, situated to the north-west.

'Annie and I were friends since we were young kids; classmates since early on in school. Basically, we grew up together. When we started dating, I was over the moon. The past eighteen months with her were great, really great. She is – well, she was – a wonderful girl. Even her parents, who probably weren't too keen on me, were decent people. Her old man wanted Annie to go with a boy who had better prospects, I know that, but he usually made me feel welcome and seemed to genuinely want to know about me and my family and stuff. I liked that about him... I just don't understand why anyone would have done this. It doesn't make any sense, you know... We had gone out for soft drinks and cake after the performance that night. I knew Mr Preece hadn't really been keen on the idea, but he consented anyway, probably because Annie had done so well in the play. She was on a bit of a high after it. We all were. There was a group of us in the diner, all in good spirits, all chattering non-stop about everything and anything. Annie and I left a couple of hours later, before the others, and went for a drive. We didn't do anything, you understand. We just wanted to be alone for a while. And then around midnight, maybe a little after, I drove Annie back to her place. I knew Mr Preece would still be up because Annie had told me her father couldn't sleep until she was home. Kind of sweet, I guess. Anyway, I sat in the car until Annie was indoors and that was the last I saw her. And now I'll never see her again.'

The Ford crossed into Ailshem, the only car on the road at such a late hour. One of the few lights visible, and the only other sign of life, came from a service station, where, the tank almost empty, they stopped to put in some petrol. The attendant was fast asleep at the counter so, after filling up, they pulled away without paying.

Annie's bedroom was tastefully painted in pastel colours. Crisp, neutral and inoffensive. Other than a school-assignment timetable and a small collection of personal photographs taped to the wall above her writing desk, the walls were bare. After returning home, she lay in bed reading by lamplight. The next day was a Sunday, a day for church, and, as was her habit, Annie had already hung the clothes she intended to wear on the back of the room's only chair.

'Here we are now,' whispered Cyril. 'This is the house.'
    Dale turned off the headlights, slipped the car into first gear and eased it forward toward the driveway; one hand on the wheel and the other scratching at his neck.

For as long as anyone could recall, the Preece family, devout Catholics and regular churchgoers, had travelled to the Sunday-morning service at Saint Dominic's in the company of their friends and nearest neighbours, Mr Norman Sewell and his wife, Susan. They took it in turns to do the driving; with Mr Preece picking up the Sewells one week, and Mr Sewell picking up the Preeces the following week. It was a mutual arrangement, often wordless, that worked well and had continued uninterrupted for more than several years.
    So it was, then, that Norman and Susan Sewell turned up at the Preece's family home at twenty-five minutes before nine.
    Mr Sewell parked his car across the drive of the Preece family home. He fiddled with the radio while his wife walked up the path toward the front door. She rang the antiquated bell, tentatively at first, a quick ring; then two more times, each one longer and more purposeful than the last. When there came no

reply, Mrs Sewell cupped her hands across her forehead and peered through the glass of the door, looking for signs of movement inside. There were none. She turned round to face her husband, who raised his hands in a quizzical gesture. Mrs Sewell shrugged her shoulders and, unsure of what to do next, pressed the bell again.

Mrs Sewell would later say in a statement to the authorities: 'We weren't sure what to do exactly because nothing like that had ever happened before. Every second Sunday, Harold and Kathryn – that's Mr and Mrs Preece – and Annie, their daughter, would appear almost immediately after the first ring. I mean, they were always ready and waiting. I never once had cause to ring the bell a second time. When no answer came, I went round to the rear of the house. My intention was to knock on the back door but of course I saw right away that the glass had been broken and the door forced in. That's when I returned to the car.'

In a statement given to the first officer on the scene, Mr Sewell continued the narrative: 'Susan, my wife, was visibly shaken when she came back. When she told me what she had seen, I made her wait in the car while I went in the house. The first thing I noticed was the terrible silence. As I called out their names, the sound of my voice echoed around the place. I made the decision to check upstairs. I really didn't like to – it felt to me like a terrible intrusion – but, under the circumstances, there was nothing else I could do. The first and only room I entered was Annie's. I noticed the blood right away. It would have been impossible not to. It was everywhere. *Everywhere*. And then I saw Annie on top of the bed, on her back, her mouth partially open and her eyes wide with terror. Her throat had been slit. I didn't need to see more than that. I used the telephone in the kitchen to call the emergency services and then I went back out the way I had come. I'll never forget the sight of that poor girl, all cut up like that.'

The police and paramedics were baffled by the sight of the three bloodied corpses.

Kathryn Preece was on their bed, a large portion of her head having been blown off by a shotgun blast. Her hands were tied with rope and her mouth was gagged with adhesive tape. The bed clothes and the furniture in the room were undisturbed, with no signs of a struggle.

Harold Preece's body was not in the same room as that of his wife's, but was downstairs, half under the kitchen table where in life he had spent so many of his leisure hours. His hands were also tied and his mouth was also taped and he, too, had suffered a shotgun blast to the face, probably from very close range.

The news of the murders soon spread through Ailshem; between friends, via neighbours, in muttered conversations on doorsteps and street corners. Death – murder, even, of the most brutal kind – had arrived among them. It brought with it a tangible sense of genuine dread that increased rather than subsided because, of course, the person or persons who had perpetrated this most awful crime were still out there, somewhere, and able to strike again at any moment.

Mrs Wilma Kasinski was among the first of Ailshem's residents to hear of the killings, the information passed on to her – rather too enthusiastically, she felt – by an elderly neighbour always eager for fresh gossip. Mrs Kasinski was aghast and her immediate thoughts were of how she would tell her son that his sweetheart was dead.

Eddy was silent for a long time as his vacant eyes stared into space. Then, very abruptly, he began to cry. At that moment, he was torn apart by dull grief and had no way of knowing that many influential figures within the police force had already identified him as their main suspect.

Ailshem, and, for that matter, Marcombe, were two parts of the wider County Police Force, which consisted of no more than half a dozen detectives of various levels of service and experience. One such detective, James Buchanan, himself a twenty-year police veteran with a respectable reputation and a clean record, was assigned as lead officer in the case of the Preece murders; largely because of his history of ably solving difficult cases and partly because he was a former Ailshem resident who knew and was known to many in the town, including the deceased.

At noon on the Tuesday, Mr Buchanan held a brief press conference in the Ailshem police station, during which he said the following as part of a prepared statement: 'There were three dead bodies in the house and therefore we are investigating three murders. The motive is unknown to us at this time. The young female, Ms Annie Preece, had her throat cut. The two deceased adults were shot; most likely by a shotgun and most likely at close range. We do not yet know how many killers there were. We are not yet pursuing a specific suspect or suspects. I am not prepared to say anything further at this time.'

This announcement to the gathered press, both national and international, was neither comprehensive nor entirely accurate. In order to preserve the integrity of the investigation, some information had been deliberately withheld, most notably the fact that a detailed examination of the house by a forensics team had discovered a partial set of fingerprints.

As Mr Buchanan was advising local residents to be on their guard, Cyril South and Dale Townsend were far from the scene of their crime. They were seated across from each other in another roadside diner, polishing off enormous plates of fried foodstuffs. On the table between them, in addition to empty and half-empty plates and glasses, was a stack of newspapers, all of which referenced the murders. Cyril and Dale had been replaying the events over and over in hushed voices and were doing so again now, willing themselves to believe they had not been careless and that press reports of a crime scene without clues were indeed true.

'There's nothin' we can do about it now,' offered Cyril. 'Only time will tell.'

Dale took a bite of hamburger. He was pensive and not in the least bit comforted by his friend's reassurances.

One week after the bodies had been discovered, an Ailshem newspaper dedicated an entire page to reporting the funeral. All three of the coffins were closed because Mr and Mrs Preece's two other children, Jane, and Richard, who led the service, had decided that the bodies of their parents and sister, in spite of the parlour's best efforts, were in no condition to be displayed. In addition to family and family friends, many of Mr Preece's former colleagues and former students, as well as many of Annie Preece's classmates and teachers, were among the large crowd; including an inconsolable Eddy Kasinski.

Rather than keep a low profile during the seven days after the murders, Cyril South and Dale Townsend drove vast distances in the same Ford car, robbing various petrol stations and small shops in isolated locations. Theirs was a life of crime – with one day often indistinguishable from the next – that would continue unabated until their arrests.

Dale was becoming increasingly troubled by what they

had done in Ailshem. His visible uneasiness and his growing tendency to vocalise his worries grated on his less-affected accomplice. 'Do you ever wonder how it is we could have done something like that?' he asked.

Cyril offered nothing in the way of a response.

Dale continued, 'I mean, I wasn't sure I was even capable of such a thing. I don't think I can honestly believe we'll be able to just walk away from it.'

But they likely would have got away with it, if Dale hadn't removed the latex gloves he was wearing in order to claw at his neck. He must have then touched something in the house, for the fingerprints from that clumsy gesture gave Detective James Buchanan exactly what he'd been looking for.

The two parolees were soon back in familiar prison garb, seated in separate interview rooms and on the way to being sentenced to spend the remainder of their lives behind bars.

James Buchanan knew Dale Townsend wasn't telling the truth, yet he couldn't help being impressed by the depth and detail of the many lies he was being fed. Had he not known better, he would have described Townsend's story as wholly plausible, even credible. He was very convincing and Buchanan could see why Harold Preece, as smart as he was, would have been fooled by whatever pretence Townsend and South had used to gain entry to the home.

'You made a mistake not paying at the petrol station, Dale,' Buchanan said.

'I've got nothing to say about that,' Townsend sneered. 'Show me the evidence or let me out of here.'

A long pause, during which both men stared intently at each other.

'You're not that dumb,' the detective continued, ready to move things on. 'Do you really think I'm sitting here with you just to talk about some petrol?'

'Well, what else is there for us to talk about?'

'How about the fact you and your friend South killed three people after knocking over their house?'

'Are you talking murder?' A derisive snort. 'Cyril and me, we're no killers. You've got the wrong people in on this one.'

'Is that right?'

'That's goddamn right. We did nothin' and you got nothin'.'

'Nothing,' Buchanan proceeded, 'except for previous, motive' – here he stopped, savouring the moment – 'and a set of prints.'

'I'm not saying another word until I get a lawyer in here.'

'Dale Townsend, I'm charging you with the murders of Harold, Kathryn and Annie Preece. You do not have to say anything, but it may harm your defence if you do not mention when questioned something which you later rely on in court. Any thing you do say may be given in evidence.'

Animism

She's the pinnacle. Of everything, not just here in Pisa. And I feel so empowered by my love for her.

She's my best friend and my lover. Very quickly after we met, I knew I wanted to have that physical intimacy with her.

To me, it touches my heart. The London Eye touches my heart and I can't let go – I don't want to – because there's, like, this pull, this magnetism about it that's, you know, irresistible.

Christ the Redeemer's my lover, for sure; who I love and who I want to be with.

It's natural. Normal. And it feels good; it feels pure, and right. For me. This is how I'm made, how I'm wired; in the same way that other people's inclinations are instinctive and innate to them. It just is.

Of course I love Harley. We have a full

relationship. And I believe she loves me, too. Everyone wants love; to have someone to love and someone who'll love them. We have that and I know we're very fortunate.

So much so that, when I returned home from my holiday in England, I immediately began making arrangements to leave New York. I've been living in London for several years now.

I'm happy to tell people about it because I'm proud of my love for him and I'm proud that he's a part of my life. Certainly, I'm not in any way ashamed of it.

You don't understand? I suppose that makes sense. Let me explain: objective sexuality is the development of emotional and physical relationships with objects. I'm objective sexual – an animist – because I feel the sentience of the things around me and I'm emotionally and physically aroused by them; how they look, how they feel, their souls. I guess it's this acknowledgement that they have souls that makes people like me different from people like you.

I first felt attracted to a motorcycle – my father's – back in high school. I talked to it in my head and it made me feel better. Then it started to become a little more physical. Yes, it did feel weird, at first. But isn't there uncertainty at the beginning of every relationship?

Rather than being heterosexual or homosexual, my orientation can be described as an attraction to objects in a romantic sense.

When I first started looking at him, it didn't take me even a day to fall in love with him.

In the past, I didn't dare talk about this inclination because there was no term for it. I'd kept my O.S. secret all my life, but as I got older I began to realise and accept it wasn't working for me in orthodox situations. I'd tried relationships and I'd even tried marriage, but it didn't feel right. So I said to myself, okay, I know what I am now. I am who I am. This is me. This is the way I'm inclined. Some people in my life accepted me. And some people did not.

No, I don't live at home any longer. My parents think I'm an abomination. They found me in an intimate embrace with my motorcycle and they threw me out. The thing is, when I was a child, the way I treated objects, and the love I had for them, was considered normal. But not now. Now it's different, apparently.

I love him. I love his mechanics and the mechanical sounds he makes. I love the smell of his hydraulics. I understand I can't sit and have a conversation with him, but he's a spiritual being with a soul and we're able to communicate in other ways. We have a bond. He knows my presence and I know his.

I feel alive when I can have moments alone with my darling. Yes, it's awkward because he's a public object and rather difficult to reach, but it's fair to say that with true love there are no real barriers.

My first was a bridge in my hometown. He was really beautiful and I found myself drawn to him. I began wanting to date him, and to date other objects, in much the same way other teenage girls wanted to date boys.

People will say is it's purely physical because there's no romance and there are no emotions. No! We have a close, affectionate relationship. I see her as animate.

We did get married last year. We're tied, flesh to steel. Like any other married couple, we're now able to touch each other whenever we want, to have that closeness. There's really not a whole lot of difference in how we do things. The joy is intense, let me tell you.

He's not a human but I communicate with him. Not in a human way; it's not verbal. It's in a spiritual, telepathic sort of way.

I knew the first time I saw the Tower that I'd fallen in love. Very soon afterwards I had a small, informal commitment ceremony to show my love for such an amazing structure. It was necessary for me to do it so I could express my love for her.

I talk to her, just like you would do with any boyfriend or girlfriend. Physically, I mostly kiss her and rub her a lot. And I masturbate, of course.

He's my world. I think about him constantly and I feel right when I'm with him.

People make sexual orientation a very big thing but really it's a small thing.

I do love her. I know people don't get it, but I do love her. I won't let go and I won't accept it's not meant to be.

Sexual orientations are much more complicated than most people think. My sexual orientation is I'm a mechaphile, meaning I'm attracted to machines. What it means for me personally is that I have intercourse with motorcycles and cars. No, I don't see myself as a tailpipe sex fiend. And yes, I'm aware it's a crime in some countries and that in those places the people successfully prosecuted for it have been put on the sex offenders' register.

One of the myths about O.S. is that the object of affection and desire is a replacement for a human. That's completely incorrect. I'm capable of having, and have had, human relationships, but they're just not for me. I decided it would be better for me to be true to my own heart and to be comfortable in my own skin. I don't miss human relationships. I don't want human relationships. And this definitely isn't a substitute.

At one point, I know I'm going to have to see her getting older and having more problems. But I'm not looking for a cure. I don't want one. We'll just have to deal with those things together when the time comes. In sickness and in health, right?

65

I think it's much easier if we can just live and let live.

The Life and Death of Archibald Smart

When I wake up from an afternoon dream – where a son I've never had, a troubled boy, pushed an old man under a Métro train as it pulled in to Saint-Michel – John Berryman is on my mind: the ubiquitous beard, his words – *'We have reason to be afraid. This is a terrible place'* – and, always, what might have been going through his head in the moments before he jumped from Minneapolis' Washington Avenue Bridge that Friday morning in January 1972. Did he think of Hemingway's final shotgun blast, as I do most nights when the bottle runs dry? Was he concerned about changing his mind half-way down, when it would be too late? We'll never know, because the only thing he had in his pocket when he took that eternal step off the girders was a signed blank cheque. That raises a worry all of my own: when the words won't come, how will I feel? When there's nothing left to write, what's the fucking point?

Berryman. The only writer I've ever heard of who didn't have empathy for the people around him. Because of this, I never could understand the man's success, which came late in life; although the pages he left behind ought to be testament enough to the depths of his talent.

The sound of the television I must have left on after stumbling onto the couch, fully-clothed, some time after most normal people in most normal places were sitting down to breakfast, brings me back to the present. The Bangles are on MTV Gold, asking if I'm only dreaming.

It's late spring, or early summer, but as I step outside on my way to a lunch date with Elsie there's a fog hovering overhead. It was there all day Saturday, too, and likely most adult days before that. I can't or won't articulate to my satisfaction why it's there, the fog, but I know how it makes me feel: regretful, unwanted, and sad.

It's difficult to like oneself when all sides are at war.

There are two things I like about Elsie: her face. She's a looker, for sure, and it's fair to say she knows her way around a cock – she once described herself to me, quite seriously and certainly expecting me to be familiar with the pop-culture reference, as *Blueberry Pancakes in the streets, Mia Wallace in the sheets* – but her weakness can be summed up by comparing her to a high school in August: no class.

And she's grown idle. Once all guts and juice, full of plans, it didn't take her long to figure out my royalty cheques mean she doesn't have to work if she doesn't want to. And she definitely doesn't want to. She has since been entirely successful in her aspiration to normalcy; now as banal and unambitious a person as I've ever met.

I knew I was in love with her even before I came in her mouth on our first date. In my book, any woman who wordlessly initiates a blowjob in a shaded transept of an empty-but-not-abandoned church, denomination be damned, is a keeper. Later that same night, she told me through tears her cervix ached but begged me not to stop until I'd fucked her unconscious. Love at first sight, she'd said just before passing out. But this was a mistake because there can be no such thing in a world where identities are confused.

We'd thought ourselves so well-suited then, as all young lovers do, but the bubbling, groaning chasms were exposed soon after we'd agreed to share an address. Many years have dragged by since then; since we first pulled those walls in around us and I said to myself it won't be long before the ashes of our relationship are entombed there. She probably felt it, too, but neither of us dared give it a name.

These are my thoughts as I'm walking the half dozen blocks to the *Floridita Bistro*. The sky above, impervious to my fog, is blue, but all I see now, with eyes wide open or closed tight, is a river of blood under a screeching, scratching moon.

Why? Because I feel like a lake that's been dredged: painful, exhausted and vulnerable.

Images from my mind's eye play on loop as muscle memory helps me wade through the pavement flesh: a length of thick rope; Plath's oven; silver razor blades reflecting in the cold bath water; my right shoe, black, pressed down hard on the accelerator into white-lit streams of traffic.

Why? Because life's too fucking hard.

It doesn't happen often now, but I am capable of being outwardly normal; normal enough, at least, to go out and eat a meal.

Today just isn't one of those days.

The head waiter, Reginald or Ronald or some such thing, shakes my hand warmly and greets me by my first name before leading us past the bar to the dimly-lit dining room, where we are seated at our usual table not too far from the empty bandstand. The suits we displace are visibly displeased about being told to move mid-meal but typically say almost nothing.

The real trouble starts when the waiter asks with a straight face if we would like a jug of either still or sparkling for the table.

'Water, Raymond?' I say. 'Fucking water?' This kind of frustration is more than clenched teeth.

69

'It's Ronald, sir.'

'I don't drink water, Reginald. And you've seen me in here enough to know that, even if you know nothing else.'

'Archie, please,' Elsie says, 'try not to make a scene this time.'

'If she can shut up long enough to drink it,' I say, 'she'll have a large white wine. I'll start with a couple of bottles of Corona, no lime. Then I want you to bring me double Stolis on the rocks until such time as you can tell just from looking at me that I probably can't spell my own surname. Which, by the way, really is Smart. S-M-A-R-T. Did you get all that?'

'What'll you have to eat?' Elsie asks over the top of her menu as I move the second empty bottle out of the way and start in on the glass, knocking somebody's shark-bone dessert spoon onto the floor in the process. Then, noticing I haven't touched my menu, she chides, 'Come on. I'm starving.'

'Excuse me,' I say, not to *our* waiter but to *a* passing waiter, 'another drink here.' I point at my near-empty glass, not looking at him. As intended, it doesn't come out as a question.

'Certainly, sir.'

Then, in an interrogatory tone that disgusts me, Elsie adds, to his back, 'We'll order now, please?'

'Certainly,' he says, turning back around to face us. 'What'll you have?'

Elsie orders seared duck *foie gras* with a grape and rye condiment.

'And for you, sir?'

'What's the soup?'

'I don't know, sir.'

'You don't know?'

'Apologies, no. Let me check with the kitchen and I'll be right back.'

'Butternut squash with parsnip.'
     'Excuse me?'
     'The soup, sir. It's a velouté of butternut squash with parsnip.'
     'That'll be fine,' I say, knowing if it's cooked right the colour should complement my salon-fresh skin.

Having worked my way through another double Stoli, I'm poised to put the first and possibly last spoonful of soup to my mouth when Elsie says, 'I didn't get enough sleep again last night.'
     I put the spoon back in the bowl. 'You're tired?'
     'Yes.'
     'Fuck sake. *I* am tired. *Me*. One more day might be too fucking much.'
     'Really? You've never mentioned anything like that to me before.'
     'Not in so many words, no.' As she forks a piece of duck into her lipstick-red mouth, I ask, 'How often do you see your shrink?'
     'Why?'
     'Because I'm thinking of getting one and I'd like to find out how it works and what works best. You know, with you.'
     'What makes you think you need to see a psychiatrist?'
     Before I can answer, a limp-wristed nobody approaches our table and asks first for a light and then for an autograph. He's wearing bleached jeans, pre-ripped, and a white tee-shirt with diamante-encrusted sleeve cuffs. Wordlessly, I take the pen he holds out and use it to scratch my name on a napkin, knowing, deciding in that moment, that it'll be the penultimate signature.

'You ask a lot of me sometimes,' I say to nobody in particular. 'I hope you know that.'

He mutters a humble thanks as he takes it and heads back to his meal, oblivious to tomorrow's value of what he's holding in his hand today.

El Chupacabra

The South Glacier, Smoking Mountain, Pre-Columbian Mexico

Lone climber Roberto Pattlin – a direct descendant of the Tecuanipas tribe who, almost three hundred years previously, in 1289, had been the first conquerors of the mountain now known locally as *El Popo* – was accustomed to strenuous effort at thousands of feet above sea level. Nonetheless, the altitude meant his breathing was laboured and his limbs throbbed with familiar aches as scolding winds whipped across the wrathful sky, displacing some loose rocks and sending spindrifts and scree down the steep slopes. The soles of his booted feet felt like stone and icy fangs bit into his gloved fingers, gnawing at them without respite. There were sharp pangs of hunger, too, and he chided himself for having naïvely breakfasted on only a heel of stale *pan dulce* and a couple of mouthfuls of running water.

It was during such arduous moments that Pattlin missed his wife. They'd got together as young sweethearts who thought they knew each other but didn't yet know their own selves. Things weren't always perfect but they worked hard to make it work well and were content with their lot, especially since recently starting a family: a son and a daughter. He thought of them as he had last seen them in the hours before sunrise – asleep, happy, safe – and he looked forward, on his return, to their excited questions about this, his latest adventure.

Climbing had been his life's passion since boyhood, but since becoming a father he had begun questioning the prudence of wilfully embarking on such dangerous expeditions. What would become of them if the worst were to happen? He had resolved, therefore, that this would be his final climb; that from the moment of his return he would remain always with the people who meant the most to him.

Pattlin decided to rest for a moment. He removed the heavy pack from across his shoulders and placed it next to him on the hard ground.

The pinch-hold ascent up the less-commonly-attempted forested slopes of the mountain's south face, from the approach to his current elevated position, had so far been a difficult yet satisfying one, filled with the technical challenge and perilous exposure Pattlin found so exhilarating. Although there remained a long way to go, he was satisfied with the steady progress he had made since setting out with the morning's silver-melting dew. That made him confident of setting up camp before sunset. He had targeted a morainal gulley less than three thousand feet from the mouth of the volcanic crater at the snow-covered headwall; its gnarled fingers reaching up through the afternoon mist to scratch at the swollen belly of the pregnant clouds. He knew better than to risk spending the night out in the open, where the only comfort would be the whistling wind emanating from the merciless jaws of darkness. To do such a thing would be to invite certain death.

In such a desolate and treacherous landscape, Pattlin naturally assumed he was all alone. However, as he was kneeling down to get his water canister, he heard feet crunching through the near-immaculate snow. He looked up and was astonished to see someone, or some*thing*, standing about fifteen metres away.

The figure looked to be dressed entirely in dark clothing. Even more remarkable than its sudden and improbable presence was the fact it appeared to be carrying no equipment with which to prevent the blood from freezing in its veins. Pattlin, wrapped from head to feet in gear he knew was absolutely necessary for survival, could not comprehend how it, whatever it was, was seemingly impervious to the bone-scraping cold of a landscape banished of all warmth.

Then, long arms swinging by its side in an exaggerated manner, it moved nearer and Pattlin felt something like an injection of ice water in the spine. He had to forget everything he thought he knew.

The thing before him was no man.

It was impossibly large – over seven feet tall, he estimated, and weighing about six hundred pounds – and looked physically strong, with broad, muscular shoulders and a thick, squat neck. What Pattlin had mistaken for clothes was in fact a matted dark fur, almost rust-brown, which covered its entire body, including the coned head and stubby fingers. The only hairless areas were its upward-facing palms and the enormous flat face. The high eyebrows were dusted with a light covering of the snow that had been falling relentlessly for several hours and sat above hypnotic, terrifying eyes that hinted curiously at unfathomable depths.

'¿Que eres usted?' asked the climber in a voice laced with terror, his words almost instantaneously swallowed by the white void. 'What are you?'

No sooner had the unanswered question left his parched lips, the strange beast began striding forward with purposeful alacrity – first over a candied stream, then a large section of verglass below a serac – and, in spite of its stooped posture, the distance between the two was quickly closed to only a few metres.

It stopped momentarily, as if pondering a decision that needed to be made. There were no external signs of this unidentifiable inner struggle; the predatory eyes under hooded lids, for example, remaining fixed on Pattlin. It emitted a guttural snort, then, with the same fluid gait, suddenly lurched forward in a swift motion that was unmistakably violent. Its speed and agility were truly remarkable. The tribesman climber did not have time to react, to perhaps reach for his well-worn mountain axe – its timber handle grooved by callused hands over countless hours of dry tooling– in order to defend himself, or to make a desperate dash for the cover of the timber line.

Pattlin's final moments were dark and confusing and dominated by a dull pain. The last thing he saw were the foul teeth in his killer's feral mouth.

Fucking Sheila

Let me tell you how I ended up with forty grand in cash stashed under my bed: I lived on one side of the law, and George thrived on the other. But we had been boys together and he trusted me.

George always had lots going on and was never short of a few quid; all of it in used notes and all of it illegal. It became routine to hold some of it for him while he was away. On business, he said.

I managed to convince myself I wasn't doing anything wrong. Besides, pals or no fucking pals, you didn't say no to a man like George Chumley.

So, my bed. Well, *our* bed. Mine and Sheila's.

Sheila. The future second ex-Mrs Dean Whitley.

The relationship started poorly and went downhill from there. We'd had another argument just before one of Chumley's men came round to drop off the loot. There's never enough money, Dean, she said after he'd left. You're a waste of space, she said. Go fuck yourself, I said, because I couldn't think of anything better. She was sore and kept going on about unpaid bills and needing money for food, so I did what I thought was right and gave her a handful of notes. The next day, with the rent due, I gave her some more. Then enough to put some diesel in the motor. So on and so forth, until forty thousand had become closer to something like thirty-seven, just like that.

Then George Chumley came back. And my whole world fell to shit.

To my surprise, it was Chumley himself who came round to pick up the bags. I told him all the dough was still there, of course, and asked if I could borrow some off the top to tide me over.

'We could come to an agreement about the repayments, right?'

'Not on this one, no.'

'Come on, eh? It's me, remember. *The Dean.*'

'It's not that,' he said coolly. 'They're not worth nothing.'

'How's that?' I asked, my throat beginning to feel dry.

'They're all fakes. Not very good ones, as it turns out. I had no luck trying to pass some of them while I was away so the whole lot'll have to go in the fucking furnace. You know, in case the cops get wind of them. You haven't tried to spend any, have you?'

Fucking hell.

Fucking fuck fuck fuck.

At that moment the living-room was suddenly infused with flashing blue and red lights. There was the sound of boots crashing up the path. Then two sharp knocks at the door. A gravel voice, 'Mr Whitley. Police. We need to talk to your missus.'

Fucking Sheila.

The Interview

'You don't have to say anything but it may harm your defence if you fail to mention when questioned something you later rely on in court. Anything you do say may be given in evidence. Do you understand?'

'Yes.'

'Okay, yesterday morning you called the main desk of a well-known national newspaper and said you desperately needed to speak with one of their staff reporters. Is that correct?'

'Yes, that's correct.'

'Can you tell me why you did that?'

'The guilt of it all was eating me up. And the shame. I couldn't keep it to myself any longer; couldn't live with what we done.'

'Why did you shoot that man?'

'I hadn't planned on shooting him, or anyone. I only took the gun along to help me get what I wanted.'

'And what was that?'

'Money. I needed money to finally get out of here.'

'Are you telling me you only wanted to rob him?'

'Of course.'

'What happened? What went wrong?'

'What didn't go wrong? The poor bastard ended up dead and now I'm sitting here talking to you.'

'Give me the details. If you're serious about clearing your conscience and getting out from under this thing as best you can, I need details.'

'Tony was supposed to go in the shop and keep the guy behind the counter busy. Then we would go in after him once the other customers had left.'

'And you, Nathan, what was your job?'

'I was outside, on the corner, ready to go in after everybody except Tony had come out.'

'And the woman, Margaret. Where was she?'

'In the car.'

'Tell me something about the car.'

'A black Ford. We had stolen it earlier that day. She parked it on the kerb, right outside the shop.'

'Then what happened?'

'Tony, for some reason, changed his mind about the whole business. I still don't know why.'

'Go on.'

'He came back out and told me straight he wasn't up for it.'

'And then?'

'Well, I still needed the money and it didn't really matter to me what Tony said. I'd already made up my mind to go through with it, so I went in the shop by myself, you know, to rob it.'

'Why did you end up shooting the man working there?'

'I'd been quite calm when I was outside but Tony's sudden change of heart put me in the nerves. I was jittery as hell when I went in. I was on my own and didn't know if Tony would wait for me or not. I didn't know if the car would still be there when I came back out. I just wanted to get hold of the money and get the whole thing over and done with.'

'Why did you shoot him, Nathan?'

'He seemed to know what was going on and came out from behind the counter when I went through the door. I waved the gun and told him to get back but he just kept coming. Crazy bastard.'

'And that's when you shot him?'

'I couldn't believe the noise it made. And the blood. It was everywhere.'

'You shot him first in the chest…'

'I did.'

'…then in the side of the neck.'

'Yes. The next thing I know, Margaret's standing beside me, screaming and crying.'

'What about the money?'

'I went round behind the counter and forced open the till. I grabbed all the notes and most of the coins and stuffed them in my jacket pockets.'

'How much was there?'

'Not much. Not enough.'

'How much?'

'Don't you already know how much?'

'I want you to tell me.'

'I think it was about forty quid. Maybe a bit less.'

'Then what did you do?'

'Me and Margaret got out of there and into the car. Tony was nowhere to be seen so we just drove away, both of us silent. I think we were numb with the shock of it, not believing what had happened.'

'What did you do with the gun?'

'I made Margaret stop the car a few miles along the road. I opened the passenger door and dropped it down a drain.'

'Do you know where? The name of the street?'

'I don't know the name of the street but I could probably find it again if I had to.'

'You could?'

'Yes.'

'And you would be willing to do that?'

'Sure.'

'At what point did you decide to go the papers?'

'A couple of days later, after it had been on television. I saw the guy's family make an appeal for information and just knew I couldn't live with myself. They said he had a couple of little kids.'

'You've decided to come forward even though you'll go to prison?'

'Yes. I know I'll probably spend the rest of my life behind bars. It wasn't an easy decision but, after what I did, I deserve what I get.'

Poster Boy

I was peering out the open back window, trying to look into the bedroom directly across from us. Sometimes the lady who lived there neglected to shut her curtains all the way and I got to see her getting dressed or undressed. From that angle, I figured she probably had no idea I was there. And I knew I couldn't be seen at all from down below, where my parents were sitting in dusky silhouette.

There were two empty beer cans on the ground and I watched as my father worked his way through a third. That surprised me because he wasn't much of a drinker and I had never seen him drink the day before a shift behind the wheel. His life was already a struggle without the added complications of alcohol that had reduced his own father, my grandfather in name only, to a mere shade among shadows. Having worked fourteen-hour days, six days a week, for more than two decades, my father, still in his thirties, had nothing to show for it except a gammy hip and a mountain of unavoidable debt he would never be able to get rid of.

My mother, at forty, looked older than her years. She was dressed in a long-sleeved blouse and a full-length skirt, with a soft hat on her head. She was using the ringed fingers of her left hand to fiddle with something white and red hanging from the closed palm of her right hand. Rosary beads, of course.

They were close together, their faces almost touching, deep in conversation.

'We need to wait and see what the doctor thinks,' my father said, lighting a cigarette. 'Nothing else we can do.'

'I know that. I'm just glad I went and got it checked as soon as I noticed the lump,' said my mother. 'Can you imagine if I hadn't gone and got it checked? God forbid.'

83

She blessed herself twice.

He waited half a cigarette before answering, 'I know. Jesus. I don't even want to think about it.'

'I'll keep saying my prayers and I'll light a candle to St. Anthony when we go to mass again this week.'

None of what they'd said made much sense to me.

My father put his can down, the crude tattoos of black crows that covered both wrists clearly visible even from a distance, and leaned over to give my mother a peck on the cheek, then a long kiss on the lips. It was one of the few times I ever saw any genuine affection between them, making that glimpse as troublesome as it was rare.

I closed the window and went inside. I'd forgotten all about the neighbour and the prospect of some forbidden flesh.

The following day, a Friday, was a big day at school. I'd been worried about it.

Lined up along the wall outside the school nurse's office with the rest of the boys in my class, I glanced around and saw they were all as terrified as I was. Rumours had been going round for weeks about what was going to happen. Still nobody knew for sure but I had heard enough to have a fair idea.

We were in for the dreaded cold-spoon test.

We were to be taken in to see the nurse one at a time. We were to take down our trousers and pants when she told us to and she would then place a spoon on our testicles. The spoon lived in the fridge. If you got an erection while the cold spoon was against your testicles that meant you were a homosexual and you would be put in a special class with other boys who were also homosexuals.

My main concern was how I was going to avoid getting an erection while naked from the waist down in a room with a woman. It didn't seem possible. Also, I was confused about how getting turned on in front of a woman made you gay but there were all sorts of things I didn't really understand so I put it down as just another one of those.

The line was getting smaller and smaller. I was getting more and more nervous.

The boys who had come out were grinning and giving the thumbs up and they teased those of us who had still to go in. They must have passed the test, I thought. They were definitely straight, then. Lucky bastards.

Before I knew it, it was my turn.

I shuffled in and my heart sank: the nurse was gorgeous; a real piece of work. No wonder they called it a test. I was already starting to feel a little turned on, still fully-clothed, and hadn't even seen a spoon yet.

'Don't be shy,' she said in a posh accent that definitely wasn't local. 'Come right in and take a seat.'

I sat down across from her in the only chair.

'Your name is Leonard Tootle, is that correct?'

'Yes, Miss.' My mouth was stale. I could hardly get the words out. 'But most people just call me Lenny.'

'Right. And what is your date of birth, Leonard?'

'Seventh of the twelfth seventy-eight, Miss.'

'Okay, if you could just get yourself ready while I give my hands a quick wash.'

She turned to face the sink.

'Yes, Miss,' I said to her back.

This was it. The moment of truth.

I pulled down my second-hand trousers and threadbare pants and stood there trying not to get an erection. I decided to do what one of the other boys had suggested by thinking of something else: I closed my eyes, waiting for the feel of metal, and began thinking of Celtic's legendary double-winning 1988 centenary team.

Bonner, Morris, Whyte, Aitken, Burns...

I'd got as far as Paul McStay when the nurse started shouting, 'What on earth are you doing, boy? Have you gone completely mad?'

I opened my eyes. She was facing me now, looking at some fixed spot over my shoulder. I couldn't see a spoon.

'I'm sorry, Miss. I thought...'

'I am sure I don't care what you thought. Put that thing away at once, young man.'

As it turned out, there was no such thing as the cold-spoon test. I was there to get a jag. A vaccine against tuberculosis, she explained. No wonder the boys before me had come out with big smiles plastered all over their faces. Either they had been in on it all along or, more likely, they were just as relieved as I was.

After the initial shock had worn off and my genitals were safely tucked away, the nurse was actually fine about the whole thing. She made a little joke of it and then let it go at that. No doubt she has had to deal with a lot worse before and since. She jabbed me in the top of my left arm with a great big needle – this caused a temporary raised blister and I still have the scar – then gave me a sugar cube to suck on and sent me on my way with a promise not to tell anyone about what had happened.

I was glad I wasn't in trouble and couldn't get tuberculosis and I felt very relieved I wasn't a homosexual, but I didn't come out of there laughing and joking the way the others had done.

Never mind cold spoons and contagious diseases and sexuality. I had a much more sinister thing on my mind. I'd looked the other way as the nurse was sticking me and some information on what girls should do if they noticed a lump caught my eye.

I'd just found out from a poster on a wall at school what my parents' conversation had been about.

Drown Your Sorrows

I heard him before I saw him.

'Rachel, is that you?' he asked.

Turning round on instinct, I came face-to-face with the man I had shared three years and a front door with.

He smiled *that* smile as the recognition was confirmed.

'Hello, Simon,' I said.

He hadn't changed since we'd last seen each other. The same handsome features, cropped hair and bullish neck on broad shoulders that he liked to have massaged by familiar hands. The same impossibly-blue eyes. The same person who'd eventually admitted to fucking my late sister in our bed while I was at work.

We exchanged the usual pleasantries and I found myself agreeing to meet him for a drink the following evening at a pub we both knew from back in the day.

I made sure to get there early and ordered the first of several rounds of drinks: bottled beer for him and what he wrongly assumed was rum and coke for me. Simon could still put them away faster than anybody else I'd ever met and this time I didn't complain. If he heard the heated exchange between the couple seated in the only booth and saw the caricature drunk asleep at the bar, his head in a puddle of spilled lager, he didn't let on.

'Let's go for a walk along the quay,' I suggested after a couple of hours, 'just like old times.'

'Sure,' he readily agreed, as I'd known he would.

The riverside flats loomed over the water that, down below, was beginning to wind its way toward the distant ocean.

It wasn't long before his legs disobeyed his intentions and began giving way beneath him.

All it took was one well-timed push and he was struggling without success against the cold and the current, his drugged limbs too weak to save themselves. I watched, absorbed, near orgasmic, until the thrashing stopped.

Then I walked away and didn't look back.

May they rot in hell, I thought as I walked into a different bar to celebrate with a proper drink.

South of Westermarck

On my way home as the sound of an approaching storm got louder and knowing I wouldn't make it before the clouds opened up with typical biblical intensity, I took shelter in an old lock-up about a quarter mile from where I lived with my mother. The large space was dark so I didn't notice right away that I wasn't alone. There were two people in there with me and, as my eyes adjusted, I saw one was a boy of about fifteen and the other was a girl new to double digits. My classmate Carl Lee and his sister, Rhonda.

Carl was stood up straight, trousers and pants handcuffing his ankles, the sweat from his brow dripping onto Rhonda's spine. She was absolutely naked, chin tucked into her chest-without-breasts, backing up against her only sibling to meet his thrusts.

I'd been there near to a full minute before they noticed me. It was Rhonda who looked round first. The smile on her face was unmistakable. Carl saw this and turned to see me, 'The fuck you lookin' at, huh?' he panted through gritted teeth. 'You want somethin'?'

I didn't say a word, just edged out without taking my eyes off them until I could feel the rain on my back. Then I turned and ran home as fast as I could, thunder ringing in my ears. The bolts of lightning temporarily scarring the sky were not bright enough to illuminate for me what I'd just witnessed.

Mr Capone Was Our Milkman

'You gotta have a product that everybody needs every day. We don't have it in booze. Except for the lushes, most people buy only a couple of fifths of gin or scotch when they're having a party. The working man laps up half a dozen bottles of beer on Saturday night, and that's it for the week. But with milk! Every family, every day, wants it on the table. The people on Lake Shore Drive want thick cream in their coffee. The big families out back of the yards have to buy a couple of gallons of fresh milk every day for the kids. Do you guys know there's a bigger mark-up in fresh milk than there is in alcohol? Honest to God, we've been in the wrong racket all along.'

Almost twenty inches of snow had fallen in less than forty-eight hours and four-foot drifts had brought parts of the city to a near stand-still. The wind coming off Lake Michigan was enough to cut a man in half.

Alphonse Gabriel, as he was almost never known, was holed up, away from such externals, at The Four Deuces; unarmed, as always, but with a bodyguard at each elbow, loaded Thompsons ready by their sides.

'A little late in the season, no?' Adelard Cunin asked the room.

'Unusual for such a thing east of the Mississippi, sure,' Al said, the words muffled because his chin was tucked into his chest. This was a habit he'd started in order to hide the three-slash scar on his left cheek, a permanent reminder of a tussle in the early days outside a dive bar on Coney Island with Frank Gallucio, now deceased. 'That's how come nobody but us is prepared.'

'I hear you,' Cunin said, 'but what you've suggested, I don't get it. Surely we should be putting everything we have toward making money before they repeal Volstead? Business as usual, as much as we can while the going's still good, you know. This sort of thing, slopping through the snow to put milk on strangers' tables, in children's mouths, wouldn't get the green light if Torrio was still in charge.'

'Johnny ain't around the rackets no more. That big prick Colosimo, neither. You gotta deal with me now, *capisce*?'

No answer.

Al raised his head and fixed Cunin with a stare. *That* stare. '*Capisce*?' he repeated, almost in a whisper.

'*Si*, Alphonse,' Cunin said. '*Si*. I understand. Of course.'

'I knew you would.' Al paused, took a sip of his Templeton. It must have gone down the wrong way because he coughed, a reflex, and some of the drink dripped out of his perforated septum, a result of years of cocaine abuse. The room saw it but said nothing. 'The newsmen are saying milk deliveries are down forty per cent. It's got so bad already there's talk of a milk famine. You fuckin' believe that? A *famine*, for Christ's sake. In this day and age. Well, I refuse to stand still for such a thing. It ain't goin' to happen here. Not in my city. Not on my watch. I came here from Brooklyn with no more than a handful of notes in my pocket, my folks off the boat from Angri with less than that even. Point is, I can't stand to see anybody hungry or cold or helpless because I know what it means to be poor, to go without. I don't want that for nobody, especially kids from this neighbourhood. There's a lot of people got me pegged for one of those bloodthirsty mobsters you read about in storybooks. The kind that tortures his victims, cuts off their ears, puts out their eyes with a red-hot poker and grins while he's doing it.' Another pause. Another go at the Templeton, this time without the nasal discharge. 'Now get me right. I'm not posing as a model for youth. I've had to do a lot of things I don't like to do, but I'm human. And I've made plenty of money here, supplying a popular demand. So, before I end up in the gutter punctured by machine-gun slugs, I want to give a little something back, show people I'm not as black as I'm painted. This blizzard's my chance.'

'And after?' Cunin again; direct, but less forceful.

'I'll tell you, when this thing's over and done with, after we've mobilised our trucks and got them through the snow, me and Mae and the kid'll go down to my place in Miami, get us some sun on our bones. And once the snow's melted, people will still want to get wet, and my outfit'll be there to give them what they want.' He stopped talking long enough to drain his glass. 'Right, I want some food with this rye before the Metropole closes for the night. We'll see each other again tomorrow morning at Meadowmoor Dairies. Nine sharp.'

'Sure thing, Al,' Cunin said, nodding.

'And one last thing.'

'Yeah?'

'You can see I've got a heart in me, but don't mistake my kindness for weakness. If you do, this kindness, me sorting out the city's milk, it ain't what you'll remember about me.'

Alphonse Gabriel got up and left without so much as a backward glance, the collar of his tailored coat pulled up against the cold; the only thing in Chicago impervious to his presence.

Only Child

We turned forty together on last December's first Friday. It was as old as he'd ever be, and this means I am now the eldest. I can say I never wanted or needed this, never yearned or in any way wished for it. I can say this because it's true. But, in a terrible parallel of my distant impotency the day it happened, the day all our lives changed forever, there's nothing I can do about it.

The day it happened. *That* day. The world fell away beneath me when it was confirmed, – no longer missing, definitely dead – as if I was being forced to pay the ultimate price for eavesdropping on someone else's nightmare. What must he have been thinking in those final moments as the ground shook beneath him? As the passenger train, on time, approached on shuddering tracks at a speed I'm sure the noise told him was fast enough? I don't know. Will never know.

I do know he walked blindly towards death. Blind, because he had so much and so many to live for but couldn't see it. There is no doubt in my mind that nobody wanted him to die; that everybody who has learned of and begun mourning his loss would choose to have him here, now. Alive again. No matter what.

He was far from perfect and would not want to be remembered as a saint. As I do, as we all do, he had flaws, dishonesty likely chief among them. For sure, there was darkness. But he, our gentleman giant, our superhero without a cape, was almost always warm and caring, bright and charming. Generous. Impressively creative. *Full of love*. Yet we have to assume he'd convinced himself it was better to die; that he believed the lives of the people around him would be unaffected or improved by his permanent absence. This is speculation, of course – the words he left behind could never be enough – but the sum total I've calculated here can't be too far away from the unknown truth of the missing parts.

He exists now without place, outside of time, in memory only. For our hearts, although figuratively broken, are in reality nothing more than beating organs, not strange rooms that house snapshots and grief. They're not where our love lives. He's certainly not, as some have suggested, even to my face, in a better place. No rational person would choose to lie shoeless in a wooden box that's about to be burned to meaningless ashes. Nobody. Not an engaged-to-be-married father of three beautiful sons. Certainly not my twin brother.

This situation – his death, our grief – will never simply exist as a natural fact. It will always require adjectives. And so it is that we, those who knew and adored him, are left to trudge towards the quiet, bitter nostalgia of middle and old age, reaching numbers he chose not to and passing milestones, acknowledged or otherwise, he likely never knew existed. All I can do – me, the man I know they refer to as his widowed father's remaining son – is move forward – slowly, with great care – in my own way, my own world, daring to turn around and look back only when my mind – for so long, before and since, a dark and unspeakable burden all its own – tells me it is safe to do so. It is then that I will be able to grieve; will be able to take cheap pride in the fact I knew and perhaps was loved by him. But not now; not yet. For the moment, I'm busy trying to tell myself I'm no more to blame for his death than he was.

Telling myself this is impossibly difficult. There's definite guilt. There are concrete regrets. Ifs and buts, maybes that cannot be satisfied. Questions without location that will never be answered, no matter how many times I ask them. Probably I did what I could, but I doubt it. Honestly, I

don't believe it. And I won't believe it every day for the rest
of my life, however long that may be.

View from the Cab

I'd heard stories from other drivers who'd seen and experienced it, including my old man, and I'd heard of drivers who'd chucked the job after one because they couldn't face getting back in the cab. So I knew the score as soon as I saw him, black cap pulled down low over a thick beard. A big lump, he was. He climbed over the perimeter fence as if it wasn't there. I pulled the emergency brake, blew the horn, shouted and screamed. But at that speed, with only a few hundred feet between sight and impact, the train won't stop in time. It can't.

There's a horrible moment of inevitability when the whole world slows down because you know what's about to happen. You know what's about to happen and there's nothing you can do about it. You sit and wait. There's no sound, no obvious noise or sign to tell you it's happened. That he's dead. But you know. And the passengers, most of them, especially in the forward coaches, they know it, too.

Your training kicks in then and everything after that is automatic, senseless, as if some other person in some other place is moving and talking on your behalf. To the passengers, the depot. The police. Then all you can do is sit and wait, again.

It was several hours before I was able to go home, but that didn't bring any relief. Any distance. My wife – and we've been together nearly twenty years, married for ten, a very close relationship; a good, strong marriage – has no idea what my job involves, not really, so I couldn't even begin to tell her what had happened, never mind how I felt about it. Sure, I got a doctor's line that was good for a wee while and the rail people – you know, the higher ups – probably did everything they could, but eventually I had to go back to work. You can't pay the bills with anger. The dead person used my train to do something terrible. His head must have been in a dark place for him to even think about doing something like that and I feel sorry for his family, for the people he left behind – I found out at the coroner's court he had a wife and young kids – but he didn't give a fuck about me; about my life and what I'd have to deal with after. You ask me, it's a selfish way to do it, for sure.

And there's guilt, too. People are always surprised when I say that, but it's true. Sometimes I have to remind myself it wasn't me who killed him. I know there's nothing more I could have done, but I still feel bad about it.

The job's never been the same since. Neither have I, not really. Probably never will be. It's not as bad as it was after it first happened. It's definitely less raw. But I'll never forget it. I remember it, all of it. Every moment. Every detail. I'd forget it if I could, but I can't. I won't.

26 Weeks

'You love me?' she says, the words falling out of her sex-flushed face turning Alastair's statement into a question and making it sound ridiculous, even dirty, and him seem foolish.

'Yes. At least, I think I do.'

Alastair concentrates on the sweat on her forehead instead of looking at her mouth as she says, 'Then why won't you offer to pay for it?'

The thrill of his orgasm still recent enough to make him confused by the tone of this conversation, Alastair comes back with, 'Because you can't be certain it's mine.' A pause as he wipes his still-dripping cock on what he thought was the sheet but is actually her leg. 'Right?'

She doesn't say anything. Her blissed look is now fully gone, replaced by what he interprets as mild discomfort. She probably needs to pee – they almost always do, or say they do – but Alastair wants an answer first. Again, 'Right, Elizabeth?'

'Yeah, I guess,' Elizabeth lies.

That's all he needs to hear. Vindicated, he gets up before she can, his bare feet slapping on the tiles as he stumbles to the bathroom, where he takes a long piss; one hand holding his dick and the other lighting a Mayfair.

'That seems like a lot of money for car repairs.'

'It does?'

'Sure. I mean, I have the money and I don't mind lending it to you, but first I'd like to know what you're going to use it for.'

'Can't you just accept what I'm saying and give me the money anyway?'

'I suppose I could, but…'

'But what?'

'But I don't want to.'

'Okay, fine,' Alastair says after a frustrated sigh. 'It's got nothing to do with the fucking car.'

'Then what's the money for, Alastair?'

'An abortion.'

'Oh, congratulations. Although I must say you don't look very pregnant.'

'Funny.'

'Is it, really?'

'Fuck no, Chester. I'm in a spot here. Neither solution is exactly favourable – having it or not having it – but this is the situation she and I find ourselves in and we have to make the best of it.'

'Never mind all that. Tell me something I don't know.'

'Like what?'

'Her name, for one.'

'Fucking hell. What difference does that make? Are you going to help me out or what?'

'What's her name?'

'Seriously, what difference does it make?'

'If I'm going to pay for it, I'd like to know her name, at least.'

'So you'll help me?'

A long pause. Chester takes a sip of the vodka that's been sweating on the table. 'Well,' he asks again, 'what's her name?'

'Elizabeth.'

'Elizabeth who?'

'Elizabeth the mother of two who's married to the most dangerous bastard we know, that's who.'

'Not Elizabeth Van Butyn? You knocked up Clement Van Butyn's old lady?'

His silence gives assent.

'You stupid fucking moron,' Chester chides. 'You absolutely fucking idiotic bastard. Let's say I do give you the money: if I were you – and, believe me, I'm thanking a Christ I definitely don't believe in that I'm not – I'd use it to buy a new identity – a good one – and a one-way ticket across the fucking Atlantic to fucking Nowheresville, U.SA.'

'What, and leave her alone with him in that house? No way.'

'*Their* house,' Chester says, correcting him.

Alastair takes a fresh Mayfair from his pack and lights it, inhaling deeply. The smoke tumbles out with the next words he speaks, 'He treats her like a cunt, you know. Demeans her. Beats the shit out of her. She's more a slave than a spouse.'

'*His* slave.'

'Fuck this,' he says, stubbing out the barely-smoked cigarette as he gets up from the table, 'and fuck you, Chester Paterson.'

Next day, Chester drives over to Alastair's flat with a wad of used notes big enough to choke a horse. And he takes it with him when he leaves a couple of minutes later because money's no good to a corpse.

Chester sees her around town now and again. The daughter. Alastair's daughter. The kid Chester almost paid to have killed before she was born.

Chester wonders if Alastair would have liked her name, or even cared.

Chester likes it, her name, but doesn't dare say anything to anyone. Not about her name or who her real father is. Was.

Vanessa never has to know.

Nine Tenths of the Law

Never understand people who ask me why I robbed all those banks. Because that's where they keep the money, stupid! Sure, there's money in other buildings – all over the place, in fact – but banks hold more of it than almost anywhere else, so that seemed the best place to get some of it without slugging my guts out at a dead-end job for the weekly average of 32.2 hours.

The thing is, taking down a bank isn't like liberating funds from a supermarket or even the office safe at your local Premier Inn. Any mug could handle that. Even you, probably. Bank robbing is taken very fucking seriously by lawmen at all levels in all places. I've never taken a gun into a bank but, because the police recognise that only a person with a certain mind-set will rob a bank, I'm still considered a violent criminal. The arseholes who own the building where I currently receive my mail (one delivery per fortnight, no exceptions) treat me accordingly: green-and-yellow jumpsuit, 390-gram Speedcuffs, 23-hour lockdown. The whole nine yards.

Didn't intend on doing a 20-year bit, of course. Had a plan I felt sure would work that day, just as it had at the 6 other banks. It was a community branch with a small staff of suits and tellers. No dickhead guard. No CCTV in the car park or over the entrance. Good access to the motorway. I'd scoped it out from a rented silver Corsa (one of the most common cars currently on the road) parked across the street on consecutive weekday mornings and, judging by the amount of street traffic, figured a Wednesday, just after opening, would be the best time to go in.

That's what I did, at almost 10 minutes after 9 o'clock, dressed all in black with latex gloves – size large – on my hands and a pair of 15-denier Spanx pulled down over my face. I headed straight for the commercial teller, a fit girl bursting out of her clothes and her thirties, and, with one hand inside my leather jacket as if holding a weapon, I said, 'Empty your rubbish bin and fill it back up with 50s, 20s and tenners from both drawers. Then the deposit bags from the third drawer; the one by your knees we both know is there. No fivers. No marked notes. And no fucking dye packs.'

When she'd done this, I snatched the heavy bin from her, turned back around, and walked out the door.

It was exactly 9:14 a.m.

Got back behind the wheel of the grey Polo I'd stolen before the sun rose that morning and drove the 70-miles-per-hour maximum speed limit to a nearby parking garage. Once there, wiped the stolen car for prints, took a 5-litre tub of chlorine-based bleach out the boot and poured it all over the car's polyester interior and on the exterior handle of the driver-side door. Got in behind the wheel of the only car I actually owned – a black Focus – and drove away.

No flashing lights. No sirens. No heat of any kind as I merged with the traffic. A clean exit.

Or so I thought.

Got home and counted the money 6 times: 4 with a calculator and twice without. Each time it came out at exactly 15 thousand pounds. Not bad for barely 5 minutes' work by a guy with almost no experience of secondary-school education.

Was in the shower when I heard them come through the front door. They were in the bathroom with me before I had the chance to realise what was happening, cuffing my soapy wrists and telling me not to move a muscle or they'd blow my memories and regrets all over the granite-grey, marble-effect tiles.

Turns out a passing citizen saw me coming out the bank

with female underwear on my face and a pile of cash under my arm. This hero followed me to the switch, where all he had to do while I compulsively wiped and double-checked a very specific number of times was write down my licence plate (JPB695K) on the back of his Cub Scout of the Year certificate. The prick (age 39, roughly 6 feet, was all I heard) gets his anonymity and a 2-thousand-pound reward, the bank gets its money back, and I get 7 thousand 3 hundred days to obsess over how to do better the 8th time.

See No Evil

after Fredric Brown's *Cry Silence*

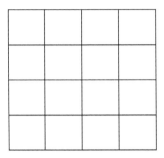

'I'm telling you there are twenty-six!' was the first thing I heard the barman say as I settled onto a stool. I'd missed my train by a matter of seconds and the bar, with its promise of warmth, seemed the only reasonable alternative to waiting on the platform.

'You're wrong on this one, Charlie,' the man on the stool nearest to mine said. He was wearing a grey coat and his face showed the beginning of a salt-and-pepper beard. 'There's only twenty-three.'

'I'm not wrong,' the barman said. 'I'm dead right. Hold on.' Turning to me, 'What'll you have?'

'A bottle of beer,' I said, not looking at him directly but over his right shoulder toward the row of refrigerators under the gantry. 'Something Italian.'

He turned round, took out a bottle, then turned back to face me. 'This okay?'

I recognised the green bottle and its red-and-blue label. 'Sure.'

He put it down in front of me and expertly twisted off the cap without having to use an opener.

'I don't see where you get twenty-six from,' the man in the coat said, 'I really don't.'

'Listen, Arnold, you say one number and I say another. Why don't we let this stranger decide?' The bartender pointed at me with the index finger of his right hand.

'Fair enough.' Arnold pushed a piece of paper under my nose. On it, etched neatly in pencil, was one large square containing four rows and four columns of equal-sized smaller squares. 'Look here,' Arnold continued, 'how many squares do you see?'

'Count them slowly, a couple of times,' Charlie said, 'then let us know how many you think there are.'

There was only one other person in the bar. A huge lump of a man with broad shoulders. If he stood up, he would probably be able to see the paper from there, I thought, but I couldn't be sure.

'Why not ask him?' I asked. 'All I want's a quiet drink.'

The two friends exchanged a glance but said nothing.

I looked more closely at the paper. I counted once. Twice. Again.

'There are twenty-six squares,' I said.

'I told you,' Charlie said. 'Twenty-six.'

'The fuck there is,' Arnold said. 'Count 'em again.'

'No,' I said, more forcefully than I'd intended. 'I counted three times and each time it came to twenty-six.'

'You fuckin' guys,' Arnold said. 'Just 'cause I'm the only one sayin' twenty-three don't mean I'm not right.'

'There are two of us who think twenty-six,' I said, 'and you think twenty-three. Why not ask the other customer?' I said again, nodding my head in the direction of the big man sitting by himself in the corner booth. 'If he says twenty-six, that makes three of us that think that way, so chances are it's right. If he says twenty-three, we can have a go at it together.'

Another glance passed between them. Then the barman spoke, his voice low, 'We're not asking him. If we ask him, he'll say he can't see nothing. He'll say he's blind.'

'Oh, I'm sorry,' I said, turning my head all the way around to look back over at the booth and ironically noticing the white cane for the first time. 'I didn't realise your friend is blind.'

'He isn't our friend,' Arnold said, 'and he sure as shit isn't blind.'

'I don't understand,' I said, not wanting to find trouble but curious in spite of myself. 'Maybe I should finish my drink and get moving. I do have a train to catch.' I took another hit, looking for the bottom of the bottle.

Nobody said anything for a full minute.

Then, although I knew I shouldn't, I said, almost in a whisper, 'Fine, I'll bite. Tell me how come you think he's not blind.'

'We *know* he's not blind,' Arnold said. 'He's only pretendin' so's he can stay this side of the big door.'

'How do you mean?' I persisted.

Charlie said, 'That man's wife was murdered a couple of years back. Her cries alerted the neighbours, who called the police. The first cop at the house found her body in the marital bed. Her throat had been slit and her body was full of holes.'

'Jesus Christ,' I said, 'that's awful.'

'A fucking tragedy is what it was,' Arnold said. His voice was low but still I felt uncomfortable. I cursed myself again for having missed the train.

Charlie continued, 'That black-hearted bastard over there was found lying on the floor downstairs, rubbing at his eyes. The cop, he put the bracelets on him right quick and brought him down to the station. He said he'd been surprised by an intruder who hit him over the head. When he came to, he said, he couldn't see anything but could hear his wife screaming upstairs.'

'And?' I asked.

107

'And the fucking jury bought the lot,' Arnold said. 'He killed his wife, pocketed the insurance, and has been walking around with that fucking cane ever since.'

'That's an incredible story,' I said.

'But he isn't foolin' me,' Arnold said. 'I'm just waitin' for him to slip up so he'll get what's comin' to him.'

'You really think he can see?' I asked.

'Sure he can,' Arnold said. 'And if we ask him, he'll say he don't know how many squares are on this piece of paper 'cause he can't see the piece of paper.'

'You're as blind as he is, Arnold, if you think there are twenty-three.'

'That's exactly right. He's as blind as me. Which is not fucking blind at all.'

Then Charlie again, to me, 'That'll be three quid for the beer.'

I put away the dregs then fished a fiver out my wallet and put it on the bar. 'Three for the beer and two for the story,' I said.

'Much obliged,' Charlie said.

Arnold snorted.

As I was putting my wallet back in my pocket, ready to leave, the big man got up in stages. Then, with the cane out in front of him, he walked past the length of the bar toward the street. I'll swear until my dying day that, half-way to the door, with his back to Charlie, the barman, and Arnold, who saw only twenty-three where I saw twenty-six, he looked directly at me and winked, mouthing one word as he did so: Thirty.

Con/Sensual

Location: London's Chinatown
Type: In-call
Duration: 1 hour
Paid: £150
Premises: Nice room; clean, warm, comfortable. Shower available. No parking restrictions.

I arrived bang on time, as I always do, because if I'm paying for an hour I don't see the point in wasting a minute. Tanya's walk-up had a typed note by the entrance: Model. Five two. Young. White. Slim. The first thing to say, that I noticed as soon as she'd opened the door, is she doesn't quite match the photos on the agency's website. The bio said twenty-four, which she would have been at some point, but I'd put her closer to early thirties, at least.

I was looking for a GFE and she'd agreed to this during our initial email contact – and did DFK, with plenty of tongues – but made it clear she wasn't up

This guy was a fucking pig. First, he arrived almost ten minutes late. Then he made a snide remark about my age. He hadn't even bothered to say hello. The only saving grace at that point was he gave me the money up front with no fuss.

I don't mind the deep French kissing, or at least I can tolerate it, but suck a stranger's cock without a condom? No fucking way! I know what I do for a living for cuddling or chatting or anything of that sort. I even had to undress myself, for fuck sake. Tanya insisted on OWC. Seriously, how many women make their boyfriends put on a rubber before giving them a BJ?

She tried to placate me by asking if I wanted to DATY – you know, RO – but I told her where to go. I ain't putting the lips I kiss my kids with near no WG's vagina; not for all the tea in China.

I didn't come when she was sucking me off so we went straight into SWO (Mish only!) and it was fine, I guess, but it just seemed her heart wasn't in it. Very disappointing. Honestly, I don't understand how you can be so obviously cold and mechanical with the men who pay your wages and expect to be in this game for the long term.

and I know how some people view that, but it doesn't mean I don't have a brain in my head. It's still my body. Clients only rent it. I have to live with it, always.

Believe it or not, most of the guys I see don't hesitate when it comes to what they call reverse oral – I've also heard some of them refer to it as 'Dining at the Y' – so I asked if he wanted to eat me out instead. But he said, and I'm quoting here, he 'wouldn't never kiss no working girl's cunt.'

Sure, I allowed him to penetrate me and even ejaculate inside me without a condom. I always do. I take other precautions and have a standing appointment to get checked every two weeks, so I have no problem giving them that much…

I certainly know what I'm doing, by the way. She had good fun with me and I think she even came a couple of times.

I'm not saying she went out her way to con me or nothing like that, but I did leave feeling dissatisfied. I've done this countless times over the years, with countless women, but none worse than her. VFM? Don't make me laugh. Overall, a very poor punt.

… but he was useless, with no technique. No doubt he picked up what he thinks he knows from porn. His poor wife! The funny thing is, when he'd finished, which really didn't take long, he asked if I'd come. I said yes, of course, but it couldn't have been further from the truth. Any punter who thinks that happens is kidding himself.

He got value for money and I got my money. I see about six men a day, six days a week, and that week he was the worst of the lot.

The Subjectivity of What We Do in Life

When he opened his eyes in the first moments of consciousness after a respiratory infection and old age had conspired to take his life in the middle of his ninth decade, the two things he noticed first were: the red-tinged darkness.

And the oppressive heat.

He had expected to be serenaded by trumpeting angels, to be greeted by legendary figures of days gone by, not this overwhelming sense of failure, this tangible fear, this suggestion that more time had been lost somehow, somewhere.

It was the painful cries of unseen creatures that frightened him the most.

I know this place, he thought.

This was not where I am meant to be.

There appeared a black-clad figure of no discernible gender, its facial features masked by the hood of a thick cloak and its long reptilian fingers dripping out of the blood-soaked sleeves. In spite of his disgust, he managed to say, 'There has been an error of some kind. How is it that I am here, in your Hell?'

'When one of you dies,' it began in response, the words falling out of its mouth sounding cold, wet, 'the God and the Devil confer to make a post-mortem decision on which eternal accommodation to allocate to you, based on how wisely you used your time in the world; a decision that always seems impossible until it's done.'

'In the world?'

'That's right. In the world, beyond the dirt. And because of that decision, you're now down here,' it spat. 'Forever.'

'But my life, what I did, how I suffered, the ways in which they lauded me, I felt sure I'd done enough to go, you know…'

'Up there?'

'Up there. Yes.'

'No.'

'No?'

'No.'

'I don't understand. Why not?'

'Because, Nelson... May I call you Nelson?'

'Sure.'

'Because, Nelson, when They get together to confer, there is of course a certain subjectivity applied to a person's lifetime of choices and actions. In your case, although in Purgatory you would have been oblivious to the passing of time, Their conference was unusually long and complex, lasting almost three and a half years from the moment of your death. The fact you're here talking to me, and not up there, talking to Him, tells us both They chose to send you down.'

'But why?'

'I have a ledger of the deceased. Next to each person's name, there is written a one-sentence summary of Their decision.'

'There is?'

'There is. Would you like to know what is written next to your name?'

'Yes, of course.'

'Born eighteenth July 1918. Died fifth December 2013.'

'And the sentence?'

'One man's freedom fighter is another man's terrorist.'

'Is that all?'

'That should be enough.'

'This is ridiculous. I am not at all satisfied.'

'With all due respect, Nelson, that is neither here nor there. Not anymore.'

'Can't I at least have the opportunity to make a comparison?'

'Go on.'

'May I inquire about Martin?'

'Martin?'

'McGuinness.'

'Ah, yes. Him.'

'Is he still alive?'

'No. He's dead, too. His death was very recent, in fact.'

'May I speak with him?'

'No.'

'Why not?'

'Because he isn't here.'

At these words, many more creatures, until that moment waiting nearby, unseen, came forward. Their long, icy limbs reached out as one and took a firm hold of the new arrival. There was no need to smother his cries of panic and rage: from his cell, nobody would ever hear him scream.

Stranger than Fiction: One

They said his words had a heartbeat, his writing a pulse. That the stuff he put on paper lived and breathed; that people read his book because he brought a certain soft musicality to a hard-boiled crime fiction whose characters were as hard as coffin nails.

But the drink took hold and it all fell apart. He could no longer successfully imitate pretence and the only remaining similarity was he still wrote in bars.

Some people said he found the bottle because he was exhausted from the constant striving. To make it. To stay there. To write the sequel to end all sequels. Others argued he had never recovered from being sodomised in the middle cubicle of a supermarket toilet at the age of ten and the dark memories of that afternoon finally overwhelmed him.

He may have had something in his younger days but when I first met him a thousand miles ago in a Duke Street boozer it was already several years since he had been considered dangerous when drunk. He was sitting alone at the bar. People were beyond him. We mostly judge by externals and, after one look at his face the other drinkers made a snap decision to disregard him entirely. This suited a man who often carried something to read so he wouldn't be required to look at the people, wouldn't be forced to communicate.

I had just finished a second-hand copy of his book, by then out of print, and had been so taken with it I decided to find out what had made him write it. A friend of mine who knew a little of the literary scene told me where I could find him. They say he's not always the first customer of the day, he said, but is there more than he isn't.

And there he was; on a stool, contemplating a bottle of lager and a rum-coke, murdering another day.

He was half-drunk or half-mad or both, but somehow tolerably coherent when he spoke. He didn't appear to be entirely lucid yet managed to digest and respond to everything I said during the hours I spent in his company that first time.

All of this was long before he was sent against his will to the sanatorium after presenting as symptomatic for, initially, compulsive giggling; and then, more gravely, the hopeless alcohol-induced catatonic schizophrenia that would lead to him hanging himself with a urine-stained bed sheet.

'Excuse me,' I began, barely above a whisper; the boldness of an urban fox I had envisaged having deserted me from the first, 'Are you Mister Graf? Mister Wideman Graf?'

'One of each,' he said in a voice as coarse as gravel, pointing to his drinks with the index finger of a shovel-sized right hand.

'I beg your pardon?'

'You want to know about my book, right? Why and how I wrote it. All that stuff.'

'Yes, that's right.'

'Well, I don't talk while I'm thirsty. It's kind of a rule I have. And I'm thirsty now.'

I ordered up the same again for him and a half-pint of house ale for myself.

After a few sips in nervous silence, I asked, 'You're really Wideman Graf, author of what was once described as the finest debut novel in a generation?'

An almost-imperceptible nod was all he gave to tell me I had found my man.

'May I ask you some questions about it?'

'As long as you keep buying, I'll keep talking,' he said, and I instinctively put a hand in my pocket to check the thickness or otherwise of my wallet.

'Okay,' I said, 'that's fine with me. How did you come up with the idea for such an unlikely tale?'

'Nobody has ever got this far before.'

'What do you mean?'

'There've been a few others like you over the years, but they shook their heads and said no when I made it clear it would cost to keep me company.'

'I understand,' I said.

'Do you promise to keep buying the drinks, provided I tell you what I know?'

My turn to nod.

He held out his right hand and I shook it.

'Then,' he continued, 'I'll tell you something I've never told anybody before.'

'What's that, Mister Graf?'

'It shouldn't really be called a novel. It's not made-up.'

'Surely that's not possible,' I interjected as he was poised to continue, the words already formed in his mouth and about to be pushed out by his tongue. 'Do you mean to suggest…?'

'What's your name, son?'

'Simeon Ledbetter.'

'Two things, Simeon. Number one: what I'm about to tell you here is a true story, every word of it, as told to me by a career villain named Bill Burnett. Bill died alone in his cell not so long ago while serving life-without-the-possibility-of-parole, leaving behind only untold wealth from his decades of capering and the ashes of a childless marriage that had lasted longer than most men live. That's why I feel able to tell this to you now.'

'That and your thirst.'

'That's right.'

'What's the second thing?'

'Don't interrupt me again.'

'I won't.'

And I didn't.

I sat and listened as the old writer told me something that, he repeated over and over again, he had never told anybody else; an account of past events that really was stranger than fiction.

TO BE CONTINUED

I Forgot to Remember to Forget

The shortness of breath and the sense of impending doom I'm familiar with – even the white stars dancing on the limit of my vision are nothing new – but the limb discomfort and the clawing ache at the centre of my chest are surely causes for concern.

I take a few steps, legs shaking, hips swaying, and soon there's a sweat on my back like a layer of frost. I'm aware of the dappled concrete under the palm of my left hand as, without thinking about it, I lean against a wall.

It's then I see him, or think I do. Tupelo's favourite son, regal in a black two-piece and rockabilly hair, beckoning me to follow. I had done so already, from that house in Mississippi all the way to the dirt in Tennessee, and I adored the journey, but am reluctant to go with him now. I stay where I am, thinking not of the music that shaped my life but of the chances I missed and the people I lost; of the skin I touched and was touched by; of life's contrasts between sunlit moments drenched in contentment and periods of crushing pain. I think also of the father I never met and the sister I never took time to love because she didn't dig the scene like I did.

I see him again, and this time I'm sure. He has a hand out, reaching for me, but I can't make out his features because the dizziness is suddenly blinding. I want to see those eyes and taste those lips, but instead I'm lost in memories of letters I should have written, cards I forgot to send, opportunities gone forever.

There are voices too distant to be clearly heard, pleading with me to do something I don't understand. I can't get to them.

I'm sitting now, or lying down, somewhere, and he's there, his hands on my shoulders, leading me to a place I don't want to know but realise I can no longer escape. There is no way to resist him now so I relent and the final dirge begins.

Mr Harrison

Timothy Smalls had recently started masturbating and, having put in plenty of practice, was already pretty good at it. He hid the sinful act under his superhero duvet most nights while his mother sat downstairs watching boxsets. He would cough his teenage seed onto Superman's mask and Batman's utility belt as he thought of doing terrible things to the slim little bodies of the girls in his classes at school.

The day it happened, at a little after one in the morning, Timothy had worked himself into a wrist-wrenching frenzy over one such girl – her mouth, the buds of her emerging breasts, legs that didn't yet know the cold of razor steel – when he was stopped just prior to the point of ejaculation by an indescribable pain in his gut.

Having forgotten all about creaming over DC's finest for the umpteenth time, he resolved to grit his teeth and ride it out. The only alternative, to yell for his mother's help while the odour of chafed skin might still be in the air, didn't seem reasonable.

But he couldn't ride it out. The pain jumped quickly from a three to a nine and Timothy called out in desperation because he didn't want to die.

The hospital room Timothy woke up in was so quiet it took him several moments to realise he wasn't alone. In there with him was a man who looked so old he was almost beyond the reach of numerical age; as if mere digits couldn't do justice to the years he'd seen.

'Hello, little boy,' was the first thing he said, and it seemed to Timothy that he'd done so without moving his lips.

'Hi,' Timothy said sluggishly, trying and failing to give a little wave.

'Oh, don't bother with any of that, Timothy. The doctor

told me you've had quite the adventure and I expect you're still tired.'

'How do you know my name?' asked Timothy, who *was* tired but not stupid.

'The doctor told me.'

'What's yours?'

'Arnold Harrison. Pleased to know you.'

'What else did he tell you?'

'Who?'

'The doctor.'

'That your mother went home to fetch you some clean clothes and comic books and she'll be back as soon as possible.'

'Mr Harrison…?'

'Yes?'

'…what time is it?'

'Well, I'm sure I don't know. It's not something I worry about.' A sigh. 'Time for me to be moving along, I suppose.'

The old man began the slow process of getting up from the chair he was sitting in.

'No, please,' Timothy said, a fledgling masturbator for sure but, all things considered, still a scared kid alone in a strange place, 'couldn't you stay a while longer?'

'Sure I could,' the old man said with barely a moment's hesitation.

They talked to each other for at least an hour about all kinds of stuff, stopping only when the old man had to excuse himself to go to the bathroom to empty his colostomy bag.

'Would you like me to call someone?' Timothy asked, sensing his new companion might need some assistance.

'No. Whatever you do, don't do that,' the old man said over his shoulder before disappearing from view.

At that very moment, Timothy's mother came into the room.

'I'm sorry to have taken so long. How are you feeling? Sitting up already, I see.'

'I'm alright.'

'Are you sure, honey? You look awfully pale,' she said, glancing at him for a moment before starting to pull clothes and magazines and grapes out of a bag-for-life.

'I'm okay, Mum, really. Mr Harrison has been keeping me company.'

'Who's that now?' she asked, fluffing his pillow and placing the palm of her right hand on his forehead.

'Mr Harrison. He's a patient, like me. In fact, he's just in there.'

'Where?' she asked, looking around the small room.

'There. In the toilet.'

'Oh,' she said, following her son's extended index finger with her eyes, 'I didn't realise you have company.'

Timothy's mother walked over to the door and knocked on it.

There was no answer.

She knocked again, harder.

When there was still no answer, she turned the handle and was surprised when the door opened.

She was even more surprised when she saw that the toilet was unoccupied.

'Timothy, dear, there's nobody in here.'

'What do you mean?'

'It's empty.'

'But,' Timothy spluttered, 'that's impossible. We were just…'

'What did you say his name was again?'

'Mr Harrison. Arnold Harrison. I've been chatting with him for the past hour and he went into that toilet to empty his own bag right before you came in,' Timothy said.

'Are you sure? They did give you rather a lot of medication.'

'It's not the drugs, Mum,' Timothy said, shouting now. 'I'm telling you his name is Mr Harrison and he has to be in that fucking toilet.'

'Timothy, your language!'

'Go ask one of the nurses if you don't believe me.'

'Now, son, it's not that I don't believe you.'

'Well, go on! Ask them!'

Timothy's mother left the room without saying another word.

'Excuse me, nurse.'

'Yes?'

'I wonder if you could help me. Do you happen to have a patient here named Arnold Harrison?'

'Mr Harrison, yes.' A pause. 'Well, we did.'

'You did? What do you mean?'

'Mr Harrison passed away.'

'Oh, that's terrible.' Hesitation, then, 'Do you happen to know at what time?'

'I'm sorry, what's all this about? I really don't think…'

'Please, it's very important. I know this must sound quite strange, but my son…'

'He was pronounced dead just before midnight.'

'Midnight? Are you absolutely positive it wasn't later?'

'Of course.'

'I beg your pardon, but what makes you so sure?'

'Because I was standing next to him when he took his last breath and I was still standing next to him when the doctor made the pronouncement. Because I've just got back from escorting his corpse to the morgue. Now, if *you*'ll excuse *me*, I have patients to attend to.'

The Emperor's Robe

It's the drink, only, preferably taken alone and quietly, that soothes me; that sweeps away the crippling anxiety and litany of regret that plague me without respite in waking and sleeping. But it grants only a temporary release, of course, which is why I always need more, more, and more again. Whenever I've stopped, or tried to, the fear and hatred that wash over me are worse than before, and so I dive in again to reclaim a level that, although not comfortable, is at least familiar.

I've come to understand this as the essence of Hemingway's deadly wheel, which I've been riding since I was a boy of fifteen. I'm now a man of almost forty-two winters and still the thirst endures. It's been my most loyal ally, my most persistent foe. Not so easy, then, to be without it.

I suspect this distaste for life drove me creatively, but it exacted a terrible cost. And I find myself asking more often: *is this it*? No matter the height of my success, no matter the choices that money and recognition afford me, I see only missed opportunities and failure; where there is reason to embrace the adulation, I experience only self-hatred and a nauseating feeling of disgust. This sense of shame – of inherent, stunted, pervasive inferiority – never lets rest my shelf-stacker soul. The bastard urban son of only a rural labourer and a dinner lady, I can never be anything other than unsuccessful, fraudulent, among those natural to the so-called better classes. It is perhaps this ubiquitous sense of being an outsider that troubles me the most.

Although this need for nervous support has pushed my brain from being damp to positively, dangerously wet, there are occasional glimpses of genuine and unfettered awareness amid the liquid madness. I know, for example, that such a schedule is a recipe for growing with the grass too soon, but am unable to rule out alcohol as a necessary ingredient.

Why? The world through my eyes is very different from the unchallenged norm, and I don't like what I see; because every moment, every gesture, every utterance, every day, is difficult, and I'm no longer able to remain vertical against the onslaught of life. No matter what I do, it's never going to be enough; it's never going to make me happy. Because I'm weary and I don't want to do this anymore. The thought of waking up to another morning where I hate myself as much as I suspect everybody else does is more than I can bear.

These are my thoughts, then, as the ground rises up to meet me in the moments before my world becomes mercifully, permanently dark.

And now I have my peace of mind.

For there is nothingness at last.

Bang, Bang

He was typically ignorant of Professor Jarry, preferring instead to spend the time staring at philosophy student Jo-Ann, with whom he shared that one class. Fridays. Nine o'clock. The only one he'd never missed.

'Edward W. Macks,' Jarry interrupted with that exasperated sigh of his, 'it's obvious to me that, as far as you are concerned, this fine morning is going to be business as usual. Why must you be so—? Oh, never mind. Wait behind afterwards.'

And that was what Eddie did, remaining in his seat as all the others, Jo-Ann included, filed past and beyond him, out the door.

When the class had gone away, Jarry began, 'Your complete lack of focus worries and infuriates me. As a medical student, you need no less than a decent grade from me to give yourself a shot at some semblance of academic success if you are somehow going to account for your time at this institution. I've already told you this many times, but these little chats of ours never seem to work. You must pay attention! I'd get you to write it out fifty times if I thought it'd do any good!'

This last sentence served no purpose because, as the words were leaving his lips, Jarry, distracted by a noise coming in from outside, turned his back on Eddie, who got up quietly and left the room without even a hint of a backward glance.

'Jo-Ann, wait up,' Eddie shouted, having almost caught up with her. 'Jo-Ann.'

'Why do you always do that?' she asked over her shoulder when he was just about level with her.

'Do what?'

'Cause a scene.'

'It wasn't so bad. And besides, it's your fault.'

'My fault! How do you figure that?'

'Well, I'd be able to concentrate better if you weren't so attractive. You know, in an abstract sort of way.'

'Are you trying to get flirty with me, Eddie?'

'Don't you know I'm trying to get a lot more than that?'

'Christ, did nobody ever tell you not to talk to a girl that way?'

'Why shouldn't I?'

'I don't know. It's… unpleasant.'

A pause before she continued, 'Look, what is it you want?'

'I told you what I want.'

'You can't have it.' Another pause. 'Not yet anyway.'

'Fair enough. How's this: can I take you out to the pictures tonight?'

'Eddie, I don't know if…'

'I'll pick you up at your house and drop you back there afterward, if that's what you want. No pressure. No hassle. And absolutely no expectations, I promise.'

'What shall we see?'

'Whatever you like.'

The pause again. Then her answer, 'Okay, yes. But I'll meet you there. I don't want my mother to know where I'm going. Or who I'm going with. I'll come up with something to tell her.'

'You do that.'

Eddie paid cash for two tickets, two hotdogs and two soft drinks.

'There you go,' he said, handing Jo-Ann hers as they took their unallocated seats.

'Thank you, Eddie,' she whispered as the opening credits started rolling; beginning, perhaps for the first time, to feel comfortable about her decision to accept his invitation of a date. And to lie to her mother about it.

This softening on her part was tragically misplaced.

When the on-screen protagonist was waging what would ultimately be a successful battle against the powers of darkness, Jo-Ann fared less well.

Eddie reached into his front-right pocket, took out a vial of strychnine – after polonium, the silver medal of malevolent toxicology – and surreptitiously put it into Jo-Ann's carbonated cola. To make sure of her death, he gave her double the dose required to cause a fatality. The effects of the fast-acting alkaloid would have felt like hammer blows on her airway and abdomen.

Her last breath was already no more than a memory as Eddie slipped, unnoticed, out of the screen through a side exit and onto the street.

As it was after midnight, the telephone attached to the wall of the kitchen where Jo-Ann's best friend, Linda, lived with a couple of other students rang more than a dozen times before she answered it. Linda, who had never welcomed the ringing of a telephone, would, after that night, positively dread the sound.

'Hello,' she managed, her voice thick with sleep.

'Linda, is that you?'

'Yes. Who's this?'

'It's Jo-Ann's mother…'

'Oh, hello, Mrs Ramon.'

'… I'm ever so sorry to bother you at such a late hour, dear, but is Jo-Ann there with you?'

'Well, no…'

'It's just that she usually comes back to spend the weekend with us but she hasn't come home yet and, as you two were out together tonight, I figured you must know where she is.'

'I'm sorry, Mrs Ramon. I don't know what Jo-Ann told you, but I wasn't with her tonight. In fact, I've been here sick for the last few days so I haven't actually seen her since Tuesday afternoon.'

'Oh, that is a surprise. In that case, I don't suppose you know where she could have gone?'

'No, I really don't. Sorry.'

'Not to worry. I'm sure there's a simple explanation,' she finished. 'Good night.'

Perhaps it's more sinister than simple, thought Mrs Ramon after hanging up. She immediately picked up the receiver again to dial another number.

The thirty-one-year-old, in the seventh month of his eighth year on the force, had pulled the graveyard shift again, meaning he spent late nights all alone during that whole week.

He had his feet up on the desk and was contemplating taking a nap when the phone rang.

'Police headquarters. How can I help?'

'I need your help. Please. My daughter is missing and I think something terrible has happened to her.'

Sergeant Pepper, having calmed the increasingly hysterical Mrs Ramon with assurances that he would do his utmost to locate her daughter, spoke with staff and students at John Moore University early the next morning.

In addition to descriptions of Jo-Ann as a naturally quizzical girl with an interest in the abstract, a girl who seemed to prefer being at home alone with a textbook and a test-tube, he also found out, from Professor Jarry, that her attention was not-subtly coveted by a fellow student named Eddie.

Edward W. Macks.

With CCTV footage from the campus' main parking lot on Roscoe Court as the genesis of his search, Sergeant Pepper then used cameras on the national grid to follow Macks' car to a cinema complex on the outskirts of the city.

He, Eddie, got out of the car alone and got back in it alone, but hadn't been in the building long enough to see a film. The officer looked again, more closely this time, and found what he'd been looking for.

'Looks like I've caught a dirty one,' he thought.

And he had.

With lights flashing and sirens blaring, he arrived to find a dead body being examined in situ by a forensics team.

Jo-Ann Ramon.

Eddie, having been found guilty of premeditated murder by a jury of his peers, stood alone in the dock as the judge began the punishment phase of the trial. 'Mr Macks, I do not agree with the testimonials – among them screaming pleas from your sisters, Rose James and Valerie Winston – saying you must go free. Thus, I would like to take this opportunity to thank the jurors for returning the correct verdict in this case. You are a wicked, dangerous young man and I have no hesitation in handing you the maximum sentence allowable by law: life imprisonment, with no possibility of parole. In your case, life will mean life. Take him down.'

Orbus

The night we met I was away on business – banking – and, without a discernible reason, had woken up in my hotel room in the minutes after midnight to find the city I would come to know so well covered in a blanket of thick snow. The kind of snow accidents happen in.

Unable to get back to sleep, I got out of bed, dressed, and went out.

The taxi driver took me to a bar he knew that served drinks round the clock and, he said, wouldn't be too crowded.

He was right. Except for two stern-looking suits seated across from each other at a corner table, the only other customer was an attractive woman around my age with dishwater-blonde hair scraped back from a face that was all at once striking and assuredly familiar.

'Will you let me buy you a drink?' she asked before I'd got fully settled on a stool; before the barman, small, with sad eyes, had had the chance to deliver his first line.

'No,' I said, 'I'll get them.' And then, as if I'd somehow caused offence, asked, 'Okay?'

'Sure,' she said, her eyes holding mine. 'I'll have a slow comfortable screw, please.'

'And for you, sir?' the barman asked, visibly less confused than I was and likely glad to finally be able to play a part.

'Whisky. Malt, if you have it. No ice.'

He poured the Glenfiddich and I took my first, grateful sips of it while watching him fix four different liquors, over ice, in a highball glass. All of this he topped up with orange juice. Years later I would make freshly-squeezed orange juice most weekend mornings for a person who at that moment didn't exist, who hadn't even been thought of yet.

Later still, I'd watch through wet, tired eyes as he sat up and sipped his drinks through a straw, impeded by a network of wires and tubes, the sounds of his laboured breathing mingling with the hum of a dialysis machine.

Kathryn – that was her name, *is* her name – and I are still together, but that early sparkle is now barely a memory. I don't know how long it's been since we last shared a late-night drink in a bar, or anywhere. There hasn't been much more than the weight of tradition and a shared experience we can't bring ourselves to discuss holding us together in the years since it happened.

If we hadn't been in the same bar at the same time, if we had never become lovers, perhaps I wouldn't have left Glasgow to be with her in London. Perhaps I would have left of my own volition to live elsewhere; Paris, maybe, or one of the many great cities in Italy. I might have married a different woman and had a different son, or a daughter, even. But those people, that possible other family, never were, and now never can be, because they exist only in that unreachable world of infinite lost possibilities. It's true to say that all the children I may have had, could have had, with all the women I never needed to meet, mean nothing to me, are nothing, because of Sean, named for my father's father, the son I have.

Had.

I had a son.

'I promise we'll do our best to look after him,' the doctor said as we, his mother and me, stood in a hospital wing not far from where I'd first heard the name of a particular five-part cocktail.

If I'd known our only child would be dead before morning, I'd have sought more robust assurances.

May he rest in peace.

Some You Win

'Christ, what was her fucking name? That blonde broad. Comedy actress from the thirties. The one that flipped a coin then got on a plane that crashed into a mountain somewhere near Vegas,' said Maurice Block, forty-four, a recidivistic gang member who had more than a decade left of a mandatory-minimum twenty-five. As a three-time felon, he wasn't eligible for parole and would have to do every day of his quarter before rotating back to the world.

'What do you mean, flipped a coin?' I asked, my voice rising at the memory.

'Just that,' Maurice said. 'She was travelling with her mother. The mother was afraid of flying so she wanted to take a train. The actress, the blonde, was in a hurry and wanted to fly. They flipped a coin and the blonde won and they took the plane. It crashed and everybody died.'

'Jesus wept,' I said, letting out a whistle. 'Is that true?'

''Course it's fucking true. The fuck I'd tell you for, it isn't true? Imagine it. Heads, you win. But actually, you fucking lose. Life or a horrendous death over the toss of a coin. And you kill your own mother while you're at it. People tell me they don't have no time for Chance, I tell 'em that story.'

A pause as we each lit the first cigarette of the day.

'Jayne Mansfield, right?' I offered.

'No, wrong,' Maurice said. 'Mansfield was killed in a car crash in Louisiana.'

'Great tits on her, though.'

'Who?'

'Mansfield,' I said. 'Fucking huge they were.'

'All due respect, Mikey, the fuck that got to do with what we're talking about here?'

'Take it easy, Maury. I was just saying.'

134

'Well, do us both a fucking favour. Don't just say. And don't you dare tell me to take it easy, either. I'll take it any fucking way I please. You got that?'

I nodded.

'Seems to me,' Maurice continued, 'you're forgetting how come you're still breathing in here; forgetting who it is keeps the vultures from your door. Do I need to remind you you've still got five of your eight years left?'

'I don't forget, Maurice,' I said, 'and no, I don't need reminding of that.'

'Glad to hear it,' Maurice said. 'Now, you know the name of this woman or don't you?'

'I don't, no.'

'Fine. What time's the library open Tuesdays?'

'How come?'

'So I can get online and scratch this itch.'

'After breakfast. Around eight, I guess.'

'And breakfast's at a quarter of seven. What time's it now?'

I picked the small shaving mirror up off the sink and held it out between the bars so I could see the clock at the end of the wing.

'A little before six,' I said.

'Okay. Why don't you come back to bed for a bit?'

'What for?'

'You know what for, dummy.'

'You didn't get enough last night?'

'Sure I did. But this here's a new day. With new needs.'

Getting back into bed with Maurice Block wasn't what I wanted to do. I'm not homosexual; and, even if I were, I wouldn't choose to fuck or get fucked by Maurice Block. I wouldn't suck his dick, either. But I knew it was better than getting fucked senseless by all and sundry every day of the week; better than getting stabbed in the shower and left to bleed to death like a stuck pig. I'd figured that out during my very first night. So I let it happen, and had been letting it happen for three years, but that didn't mean it wasn't rape.

I broke the law and deserve to be here. Selling drugs is no way to live a life and I knew, long-term, the only outcomes were the key or the coffin. But I never figured on ending up as a fuckboy in an iron cage.

That first night locked up, I was put in an empty two-man cell. As soon as the guard who'd escorted me there was out of sight, Maurice Block opened the cell door and came inside.

'Get on the bed,' were the first words out his mouth.

'On the bed?' I asked, confused. I was standing in the centre of the cell, looking at my new surroundings, trying to take it all in. 'What do you mean? It's only three in the afternoon.'

'I don't want to go to sleep, dickhead,' Maurice said. The menace in his voice was real and unmistakable. 'Now I'm not gonna tell you a third time: get on the fucking bed.'

Maurice removed his trainers and began to take down his prison-issue trousers.

'What the fuck are you doing?' I said. 'I don't know who you are, but I'm telling you, I'm no queer.'

That was when Maurice punched me for the first time. It felt like a bomb had gone off inside my skull. Then Maurice hit me again and my ears started ringing. A wave of nausea rose in my chest.

Next thing I knew, I was face-down on the bottom bunk. Maurice was on top of me, pushing my face into the pillow to silence the screams.

Then Maurice was inside me, his right forearm on the back of my neck as he pounded me. The pain was intense, electric, and I felt like I was being split wide open. The

136

weight of Maurice's muscle-bound body was crushing me; I could hardly breathe, never mind shout for help.

I managed to turn my head around to the left and saw another pair of big, hairy legs. Someone else was in the cell.

Then I heard a wet smack as Maurice pulled his cock out my arse, which pulsed with a throbbing pain. I tried to get up but couldn't. My legs felt weak, empty. I lay there, sobbing, glad it was over.

But it wasn't.

'No, fucking no. Please, stop. Please,' I yelled as another man pinned my body to the bed. I could see Maurice standing by the cell door, looking up and down the wing. Then I felt the pain and pressure of another erect penis enter me.

I cried out in anguish, felt a dull blow to my right temple that came close to knocking me out.

Whoever it was kept pounding me, and every agonising thrust jolted my whole body. I tried again to get free but couldn't.

Over several minutes the pain lessened and a numbness washed over me. I began to fade out, to drift toward unconsciousness, as the pulverising continued.

When I regained consciousness, I was still on the bottom bunk but nobody was on top of or inside me. Someone had put my trousers back on and pulled a blanket up over my legs.

I opened my eyes. Maurice and the other man were sitting on chairs.

'Tails,' Maurice Block said, flipping a fifty-pence piece into the air with one hand then catching it in the palm of the other.

'Tails it is,' the other man said as he got up to leave. 'This one's all yours, Maurice, you lucky bastard.'

'Come on, Mikey,' Maurice said, bringing me back to the present. 'I don't want to wait all fucking day.'

Mumms on Ice

My tax return stuff is spread out on the table in front of me. The telly's on low in the background and I'm faintly aware of a bunch of never-have-been celebs prancing round a ballroom in Blackpool or some other forgotten seaside shithole.

Then I hear the words that always make the tops of my ears flush with excitement: *We interrupt this broadcast with some breaking news.*

At the prospect of respite from the mundane, I put down my pen and pump up the volume as the announcer continues: *We're receiving reports of a serious incident inside Buckingham Palace.*

Dear Jesus, this could be it, the one I've been waiting for! At last, an end to being lauded over by a too-old half-German reptile and her parasitical brood of useless, patronising, money-grabbing cunts.

I head for the fridge. Can almost taste it. The cold. The bubbles. Toasting the joy of freedom with her gone forever.

Then he says it: *Although she was in the Palace at the time of the attack, we can confirm the Queen is safe and well and is now out of harm's way.*

I turn my heels to the kitchen and get on with the paperwork, the telly mute until the dancing comes back on.

Regular. Scheduled. Programming.

So close, I think. So close.

Maybe next time.

The Final Bell

He could hit with both hands and was light enough on his feet for such a big man, but the problem was he took too many on the way in. And as much as he was admired for having the heart to find his feet time and again, journeyman Pierre Robin's weak chin meant he also had a reputation for going down easier than a twenty-quid hooker. In fact, there were plenty at ringside, before and after the doctor climbed through the ropes, who said he should never have been allowed to lace up his gloves that night.

The man in the other corner had moved in under the jab at will and all Pierre could do was grab him, taking heavy shots to the ribs and kidneys each time. Pierre, through pain and exhaustion, was soon unable to grab hold. The other man saw this and stepped back into the centre of the ring, using his superior reach to land left jabs and straight rights on Pierre's forehead, ears, chin and mouth until he slipped down the ropes and onto the familiar canvas, oblivious to the count.

'That was your last fight, Pierre,' his corner man and friend said. 'You've got to give it up before one of these guys does damage you won't walk away from.'

They were in a side room off the hospital's I.C.U., where the fighter who'd never been a contender had just regained consciousness, a full hour after being knocked down and out in the dregs of the fourth.

Pierre knew it was good advice – advice he'd have to take because surely nobody would sanction him now – but, in a world where weakness could be fatal, he was reluctant to admit the only life he'd ever known was over for good.

'You talking retirement, Charlie?'

'You're out of options here. Anything else would be suicide.'

'Never.'

'Now.'

'What would I do instead?'

'Something else. Anything else. While you still can. You've been around this game a long time but still know enough to tie your own laces and remember your kids' names. That ain't nothin', believe me. And there's some money in the bank, right?'

'A little, sure.'

'Listen, you never dodged nobody and you always gave it your all. People know that and they respect you for it. Ain't no shame in hangin' 'em up now, the training you done and the punches you took.'

'And the sacrifices.'

'Of course.'

Pierre knew Charlie was right, that this time he'd have to throw in the towel for real, forever. Not even the knockout shot in his one and only stadium fight several years and too many rounds ago had hurt so bad.

Ouab Days

THE JUNKY's flat was on the third floor, closed curtains facing the street. The door in the stairwell opened into the kitchen and THE JUNKY had to pass chipped worktops to get to the living room. Books he'd never bothered to read were piled haphazardly on every surface: on windowsills, on and under chairs, on sagging homemade shelves. His only table was a mess of past-due bills and an ashtray overflowing with brown butts. Dishes were stacked high in the kitchen sink, abandoned.

Here's what THE WRITER knew: life is hard. And trying to finish a novel? Forget about it. That's the hardest fucking thing of the lot. So hard it hurts. He'd been biting his nails over that same piece of work for too long but couldn't get it over the line. The words wouldn't come and he often had nothing to show for days of unbroken effort.

He was lodging in a rooming house with high ceilings and decent-sized sleeping quarters. A stained writing desk positioned underneath the only window looked out over a litter-strewn courtyard. Adjacent to the desk was an open fireplace, packed with old newspapers, blocks of wood and used matches.

Bent over the typewriter in his bricks-and-mortar prison – frustrated, listless, depressed, his back breaking and his heart aching – he resisted the urge to let out a monstrous, guttural howl.

THE HUSBAND and THE WIFE stayed in a tenement block near the university campus. The stairs were at the back of the building, with two flats on each floor. Theirs was at the rear. A corridor led past the kitchen to two small bedrooms, then to a white-tiled bathroom with a freestanding porcelain tub. Sliding doors opened onto a sunlit living room. The only negative was there was no lift.

Their lives, happy once, had become a cluster-fuck of simmering loathing: of themselves, of each other, of the whole damn world. They could no longer imitate a pretence of shared desire and this led with increasing frequency to the thrashing-out of awkward compromises ultimately unsatisfactory to them both. Their disagreements had become more malicious; their reconciliations more rehearsed and less reassuring.

In one of many too-late efforts to put a sticking plaster on a shotgun blast, THE HUSBAND and THE WIFE had decided to socialise together on a more regular basis. With BABY GIRL still at home but just about old enough to fuck up her own life according to her own schedule, it seemed as good a time as any to give things another go; to make one final attempt at salvation before calling it quits. It had to be cheaper and more effective than that cunt of a marriage counsellor and his stupid cunt of a wig.

THE ALCOHOLIC's life was a struggle. Having worked fourteen-hour days six days a week for almost two decades, he had nothing to show for it except unavoidable debt on two credit cards he would never be able to get out from under. No family. No friends. No social routine of any kind. No car payments, either; but when you could reasonably walk to work on sunny days, what fucking difference did owning outright a set of second-hand Japanese wheels make?

It wasn't recently, then, that he had begun questioning the purpose and validity of his existence. Exhausted from the constant striving, he needed something else. Something more. Or nothing at all.

At first glance he appeared to be rather dapper but, on closer inspection, it was clear THE TEACHER had managed to cultivate his look with clothes that could at best be described as charmingly scruffy: a black shirt with frayed collar and cuffs, a stained black tie someone bought him for his first proper job, a dark suit-jacket that probably used to fit, shoes so big they were upturned at the toes, charity-shop socks. And a faux-leather belt almost as young as THE HOOKER in the rented bathroom, calling her pimp or cleaning her pussy or some other fucking thing.

The passive look on his face betrayed no sign of the heat and excitement growing in his throbbing cock, increasingly erect above the faded dark cords and cheap boxers round his ankles.

THE TEACHER failed to stifle an anticipatory gasp when THE HOOKER came back in, crawling across the tiles on her freckled hands and scabbed knees. The delicate rays of sunshine creeping in through the room's only window gilded her hair and gave the porcelain skin of her naked body an almost luminescent look.

There was neither conversation nor hesitation.

She took his shaved balls in her left hand and used her right hand to guide his cock – also shaved, and now fully engorged – into her mouth. All of it.

There was a loud groan.

A momentary religious conversion.

Considerable buckling of the knees.

It wasn't long before she was swallowing everything he had to give. His grunts and cries bounced off the motel room's plasterboard walls.

One of his big callused hands grabbed her mass of red hair and jerked her head back. He leaned down and kissed her full on the lips.

There were still no words, only light-headed satisfaction.

THE HOOKER was put on her back on the bed and, arse spanked raw, all filled up with a tongue and thick, wet fingers.

Within the hour, those same ringed fingers, balled into fists, applied fresh bruises to old make-up; energy spent and temporary reminders given instead of paying the money owed.

There it was at last, THE WRITER's river, over whose bridges he had walked and wept alone in joy and sadness all those years ago. She is finally and completely the greatest river in the world. The streets above her move and hum like no others, their pulse infinite and absolute, their energy often so great and so wonderful a person can take a deep breath and get high on huge gulps of it.

This city had had a more profound effect on THE WRITER than any other environment; the extent of this impact incommunicable to anyone who had not spent their formative years roaming its streets and absorbing its sights and sounds through their pores.

If I can't be here, he thought, I don't want to be anywhere. It's the beginning and the end and deserves no comparison.

Uncle Hugo's was a hustlers' dive that never shut. Dawn until dusk you could find every type of character in there, either propped up against the long walnut bar or huddled in a corner booth carving up the latest piece of work. Pimps and their hookers. Pushers and their addicts. Ex-cons. Careerists with eyes and ears open for a wheelman or an alibi. Bop musicians and vagabond poets washing down the remnants of broken dreams with warm lager served in a bottle or a glass. Even the occasional drug cop with his hand out. It was run by Irish Pat, a stocky man of fifty with enormous hands. Pat knew his customers and he knew the score. He also knew how to use a shotgun.

THE JUNKY was in there with Terry Snark, a double

leech only marginally more intelligent than a moron who'd sell you cancer if it meant a grain for him in return.

Pat was pouring drinks for Terry and THE JUNKY. Terry was a small-time jive artist who lived in a cold-water flat near the meat-packing district. THE JUNKY had to be careful what he said because word was Terry had gone wrong and was working with the authorities. Terry was tall and thin with long fingers dripping from bony hands. He got his habit more than three decades before and had that look: shifty fish eyes sunk back behind protruding cheekbones covered with sallow flesh. The story of a hard life was etched across the parchment of his face. His mouth drooped at the corners, giving him an imbecilic expression that was not out of place. When he was junk sick, the skin on his arms and legs twitched. It was as if in their desperation the junk-hungry cells were trying to burst out of his body in search of a fix. At those times, Terry wouldn't bathe or change his clothes, claiming the water hurt him. He didn't eat or sleep, either; using the little energy he had left to score. He didn't have the sand to roll soaks on the subway so mooched about for half a cap on credit from the latest connection or from other users he thought might be holding, either there in the bar or outside at the lunch counter.

While THE JUNKY sipped at the dregs of a weak rum-coke, Terry was pestering him for a share of the gear he imagined was stashed in THE JUNKY's coat. On the cuff, of course. THE JUNKY told him straight he didn't have any. Hearing the answer was no and hearing THE JUNKY meant it, he fell silent; the thin lips of his rictus mouth set hard as stone. With no chance of getting a hit, there was nothing left to say. Terry wasn't there to socialise. THE JUNKY moved round and watched him shuffle out onto the street.

THE JUNKY turned back to the bar and noticed a woman settling onto a stool across from him. Concentration-camp hips and deflated AlloDerm lips. She cracked open a benny tube and took out the folded strips of paper. These she mixed crudely into a porcelain cup of black coffee, swallowing it all in one huge gulp. Within minutes she had checked out; a goofy grin plastered across the rough contours of her face.

And still THE JUNKY waited.

THE WRITER wrote some useful fragments on scraps of yellow paper while sitting high above the city's rooftops; rooftops that groan under the weight of history.

'Are you anywhere?' he asked.

'No. You?'

'There's a panic on. I don't know nobody who's holdin'.'

'Can't you hook me up, man?' THE JUNKY pushed, trying to keep the urgency out his voice. 'I've got the dough.'

'How much you got?'

'Enough to put me right before the sickness starts.'

'Yeah?'

'Yeah. Just tell me where.'

THE TEACHER's senses, already alert, were heightened by the pitch black of the basement on Pulp Street, rented because of its isolation.

His palms groped the air in the small space and quickly found her silk skin. Wordless, he pushed the woman, a random, forcefully so that her back landed up against the nearest damp wall.

Her neck arched as he filled her mouth with his tongue. The fingers of his other hand, having first scratched at her breasts and buttocks, were soon wet with her.

THE TEACHER lifted her up and could feel her thighs tremble as he put himself inside her.

'Please. Please. I need to…'

'No. Not yet. Fucking wait.'

Her long crimson nails clawed wildly at his broad back. The pain of it urged him on and he gave several hard thrusts.

'Now you have my permission to come.'

Shaking and sweating, she bit his neck to stop herself from crying out. He did not show the same restraint; coming so hard he let out an almost-feral growl.

THE TEACHER collapsed onto the hard tile, panting.

That city in the early hours reminded THE JUNKY of the dawn streets of his childhood with its buildings caked with grime and putrid semen trodden on by barefoot bastards starved for attention with guts swollen on lard.

He found the right door and knocked hard.

Under the cover of a sad morning frost, as the final remnants of a monochrome night butted against emerging silver shards of unavoidable dawn, THE ALCOHOLIC could no longer resist the swelling compulsion. He chose to nibble at the corners of curiosity by imbibing a pre-work car-park cocktail can. It was an unmistakable act; a deliberate and purposeful numbing of the senses. And it felt good.

THE JUNKY chose junk only once. After that it chose him and he was hopeless to resist. He had to have it and would do anything to get it. It had become his way of life.

THE JUNKY could say he started on it during a personal crisis or to cope with the horrors of grief, but the truth is he had got bored with the usual pills and powders and was looking for the next big thing. He thought he'd found that in junk. After many long years of sordid routine, it was true to say he was where he was because of nothing more than dumb curiosity. Wondering about the unknown had cost him the whole lot.

The following morning, lathering his face for a shave, THE ALCOHOLIC regarded himself in the mirror with taciturn interest. Things were different. He had crossed the divide of a great taboo and didn't know what would happen next. Soon, maybe he wouldn't care.

NEAL-NEXT-DOOR, arriving late, blew into the room like a hurricane; his energy manifesting itself in wild, jerky movements of his limbs and in manic, machine-gun talk that was wholly impervious to the initial indifference of the people around him. He immediately settled on a corner couch from where he watched the rest of the night's innumerable arrivals and departures through dark, brooding eyes.

THE JUNKY got out his works and cooked up, feeding his arm with a bloodied spike. The familiar effect was instantaneous; first a hint of it behind the knees then a warm feeling that washed all over the body.

No more pain once it's in the vein.

THE JUNKY registered no disgust or self-loathing, only acceptance, as his addicted cells digested weak derivatives mixed with milk sugar before the borrowed needle dropped onto the tiled floor. He was soon repugnantly catatonic; swollen tongue lolling out of mouth, oblivious to the quivering, quaking ingresses and egresses of another trembling city night.

With no job and no money, THE WRITER had to find a way to survive; to put even a meagre amount of food in his belly. He knew, long-term, how he had paid the rent would be of no importance. The justification would be what he left behind in print.

Now, though, the choice was between pawning his typewriter or the watch his daughter, his only child, gave him as a birthday gift the last time he saw her.

Thick plumes of marijuana smoke drifted above the heads of people in what was a very crowded room. Joint after joint was rolled and lit and passed around by NEAL-NEXT-DOOR until it was possible to feel the effects simply by inhaling the air around him.

'What do you have?'
'Just this here,' THE WRITER said on cue, putting the watch on the counter.
'How much you want for it?'
'No, you go.'
'Thirty.'
'It's worth closer to forty. Forty, at least.'
'Where? Isn't worth no more than what it's worth right here.'
'I guess you're right.'
THE WRITER took the money and left; feeling cheated but not quite sure how or why.
Oblivious to time, he resolved to make every word count.

THE WRITER's daughter was no saccharine sweetheart in a gingham dress and white knee-high socks. She was a suitably-sly, street-wise woman. Shock-proof and alert, her life dragged along according to her own private clock: a tobacco-haze routine of pout pray panties cock.
She, THE HOOKER, limbs weary with filthy copulation,

struggled into the bathroom and, freckled hands gripping the bowl, threw up a crude mix of cereals and semen.

When THE JUNKY woke up he had no idea where he was.
In the bathroom he resisted the urge to vomit dry bile onto cracked porcelain. He looked in the mirror. Fuck it, he thought, there are no mirrors in a coffin.
He rolled up his shirt sleeve, put on his coat and left.

They hadn't seen each other for almost four years and had spoken maybe only twice in all that time. THE HOOKER knew she hadn't missed him. You don't miss something you never had. She had no real desire to see or speak with him but that black-clad trick had taken everything.
It was a call she hated to make but, with nothing left to pawn, she had no other choice.

A murder of crows stood in black silence under a heavy rain that was flooding the gutters. The pre-dawn streets teemed with barefoot women, prowl-car coppers, Benzedrine blitzers and naked mad pill poppers. He saw cool-cat hipsters smoking sticks of tea among fetid piles of animal faeces in abandoned laundries, grinning maniacally through the haze of approaching nightmare morning. He saw intoxicated juveniles turning tricks for petrol money under yellow street lights as the uniforms drove by with bored looks and coffee cups.
THE JUNKY began the long walk home.

The dark sky sagged with heavy clouds and cold rain gargled in the drains. THE ALCOHOLIC pulled the cap off and his whole sad life came gushing out.
Getting an early-morning load on made him more tolerant of the afternoons which, under the influence of a

half dozen cans of beer or a quarter bottle of blended whisky, became manageable patches of foggy half-drunkenness.

This was his new normal.

THE HOOKER should have known there would be no answer. He'd never been there for her, whether she needed him or not. Consistency seemed to be that bastard's only trait.

The message she left was blunt: I'm in trouble. I need money. Please, help me.

No longer on the couch, and his system no longer without the effects of cocaine, NEAL-NEXT-DOOR gave an even more immediate expression to his thoughts. He needed no encouragement to vent his ideas and frustrations, to divulge his innermost desires and vexations. His zest for life was infectious and he dragged people along with him through sheer force of personality. This he'd always done.

SHE had been deliberately naughty in the preceding days, going out of her way to antagonise and provoke her husband. Before leaving for work that morning, THE TEACHER had told her SHE'd receive her punishment that night.

Finally, SHE thought.

Will it be with a hairbrush, one of my books, the leather strop he uses for shaving? Or some other instrument of pleasure, as yet undiscovered?

The hours crawled by as SHE wondered about it.

THE ALCOHOLIC woke up slowly a few minutes after ten o'clock. The flat was in utter disarray which, in the cold morning glare, seemed almost criminal. He needed a bracer. His hands were unsteady as he lit a filter-tip

151

cigarette from someone else's pack with someone else's lighter.

THE TEACHER arrived home at the usual time and, without saying a word, placed the razor strop on the dining table. SHE shivered with excitement at the sight of it, recalling the large red welts it had left her with when he last used it several months ago.

'Take your clothes off,' he growled, 'and get on the fucking table.'

SHE quickly undressed.

Face-down over the table with her feet still on the floor, the wood was cold against her naked, sweating flesh. He blindfolded her with one of her silk scarves.

Her skin was tingling and SHE was already wet with anticipation. He sensed this and, mercifully, didn't make her wait long.

Once. Twice.

The coarse leather struck her buttocks three times in quick succession.

SHE bit her lips to stifle a cry and the metallic taste of blood filled her mouth.

Four. Five.

The pain was delicious, sending electric sparks up her spine and down the backs of her trembling legs.

Six. Seven. Eight.

SHE lost count and was soon drifting in a semi-conscious world of pleasure as the stinging jolts continued unabated. Her painted nails dug into the table, marking the wood.

Shouts filled the room. The noise urged him on; the frequency and force of the blows increased.

Just when SHE thought SHE couldn't tolerate any more, the thrashing stopped.

Her arse was stinging, her body shaking. Her hair dripped with perspiration.

In the moments immediately after the blows had ceased, all SHE could hear was his panting from the effort of such a tremendous spanking.

Then there was the noise of his zip being undone and SHE felt the full weight of him; on her, then inside her.

One thrust. Hard. Deep.

Two. Three.

More.

SHE still couldn't see but SHE knew there was a rare smile on THE TEACHER's face.

Without intending to, THE WRITER found himself seated at his desk, hands poised delicately above the typewriter. He read the words of the night before and, dissatisfied with their puerility, yanked the sheet out and tossed it into the wastepaper basket.

Today, he thought. It has to be today or not at all.

THE ALCOHOLIC lulled about in the melancholy emptiness, feeling listless and detached; trying without success to piece together the various happenings of the night before. A dreary light filtered in through the open window.

THE JUNKY was alone in a corner booth of Hamburger Mary's, quelling his morphine hangover with milk highballs. Having chosen fuel over food and arrived hungry, he swapped first-draft poetry fragments for stale margarine sandwiches.

Sullen-faced men and women sat in the other booths, the drone of their conversations barely audible above the jazz records blaring out the jukebox. He could make out occasional snatches of existential gibberish infused with an unnecessary urgency.

THE JUNKY sat there, lost.

A fever-induced ecstasy of the mind and an imperishable compulsion for literary success caused spontaneous prose to gush out of THE WRITER in the bright confusion of early dawn.

Soon, the final draft of his first novel was almost finished. At last.

THE HOOKER, broken-down and beat, pursed her lipstick lips in grim anticipation of the night ahead. Her skin ached and swelled with black eyes and alleyway bruises. Soup and sodomy were sure to be on the menu. Naked flesh would be chewed, slurped, eaten; and she would soon be choking on punters' rusty cocks and on her own straight-jacketed dreams.

THE TEACHER's cheekbones ached because SHE was sitting on him. The matted fist of her pubic bone had been punching him in the face for who-knows-how-long.

He gave her arse a last grope, then pushed her hips backward, suddenly swallowing air instead of milkshake-thick mucus. SHE moved backward, looking to sit on his semi-hard cock.

'Wait,' he said, 'I'm thirsty.'

'You're thirsty?'

'Yes. I'm not sad or angry or lonely. I'm not craving a smoke and it's been maybe four days since I felt hungry enough to eat. But I've just spent unknown minutes drowning in the dark and now I need a drink.'

In the kitchen, THE TEACHER filled a highball glass half with whisky and half with water and drank it down. Then another.

Back on the bed, SHE was on her hands and knees and he was deep inside her. It was not as tight as he remembered but it was good enough. He pounded hard, the opposite sides of their hips bones cleaving together, parting, cleaving together again. It sounded like a cheek being slapped.

THE TEACHER's objective was to give her urethral sponge something to soak up. This happened sooner than he'd have liked, but not so soon that she was pissed off.

Once it was over, he wanted to tell her to get out; that he'd call her a taxi. The words sat on the tip of his teeth, waiting to be pushed out by his tongue. He could feel the weight of them in his mouth.

'What is it?' SHE asked.

'You know I love you, right?'

Hollow-cheeked, ignorant of greasy pieces in kebab-shop salad bags, THE JUNKY stared at a stain on the wall for nine hours and all he could see with those vacant eyes in the dregs of gear amid the piles of brown needle ash were broken souls, primordial visions, silent screams and monochrome dreams. Only the mud in the vein, he knew, could slake the insane hunger gnawing at his bones.

She rarely said no. A prostitute who won't turn tricks is hardly pushing an ideal business model.

But that night she'd said no and she'd meant it.

THE HOOKER had been in some fucking back-of-beyond hourly-rate room but something was off and she told him to forget it. Mutual time but no money wasted. Sorry for the inconvenience. I'm sure you understand. All that bullshit.

No harm, no foul, right?

Fucking wrong.

He wanted to know what kind of shit she was trying to

pull. 'What is the world coming to,' he said, 'when you can't even pay a woman – A FUCKING WHORE! – cash money to swallow your load? I'll show you.'

And he did. Twice.

Once in the front with his limp dick. No condom. Once round the back with an empty beer bottle. No mercy.

'That's what the fucking world's coming to,' he said. 'How do you like that?'

Itching to get the monkey off his back, THE JUNKY hustled in the plunging dusk for a sympathetic chemist willing to fill an ill-gotten prescription but they were all burned and he couldn't get hold of synthetic H or even diluted M from his old wholesale connection so he had to make do with codeine and two strips of benny that didn't even begin to scratch the surface of the awful junk sickness in a night as fathomless and unforgiving as prison darkness.

THE HOOKER didn't leave a message. After trying the number four or five times in the space of twenty minutes, she gave up.

THE WIFE usually couldn't tolerate having strangers in such close proximity. It accentuated her hard-wired nervousness, making her absurdly skittish. Why, then, was she able to babble confessions at this man, this NEAL-NEXT-DOOR? What was it about him that made her feel an irrational compulsion to tell him things she would never dare utter, even to her HUSBAND? His permanent manner was an affected one of exaggerated politeness and when he spoke, although it was very fast, he did so as though condescending to explain something to someone of a lower intellect. Yet even this didn't bother her.

As she reapplied a layer of siren-red to lips so raw from his stubble it hurt to touch them – as her other lips would later hurt when she urinated – THE WIFE asked herself what had made her do it?

A watch was no use to him: he was running on junk time. Leaning heavily on the mahogany bar, his eyes drowsy from a Nembutal sleep he didn't remember, THE JUNKY scanned the crowd and saw after-dinner cigarettes being lit with borrowed matches, a beer drinker chasing his familiar lush kick, and a whore wearing a goofball grin whose reptilian pimp was spitting cotton into his glass.

All of this while THE JUNKY waited in muted horror to cap some Mexican shoe scrapings; just another dope fiend aching for his skin to jump with those delicious prickles.

As he typed the final words of the final chapter, THE WRITER was surprised by the utter lack of elation. He had expected self-satisfaction; to be pleased at finally being free from the constraints and pressures the manuscript had come to represent. The guilt he had endured at not being able to bring it to completion was replaced by a guilt for all the time he had spent agonising over it.

That, too, would soon give way to a curious emptiness.

The significance of the moment did not occur to him until much later, by which time it was too late to appreciate.

It did release him to indulgent leisure, though, and no sooner had the ink dried on the last word than he, a man who had never welcomed the ringing of a telephone, was engaged in near-frenzied dialling and rushed conversations in order to arrange a gathering at his home. Some of them, he later realised, were people with whom he had had barely more than a passing acquaintance and whose numbers he had no memory of having acquired.

SHE was still at work. The escort service didn't open until ten. No girls on the streets yet. No answer at the number that was usually so reliable. And online porn was all about black dicks and hairy chicks these days.

So THE TEACHER chose fruit. Because fruit was a sure-thing that didn't give you any shit or expect a tip.

He used a screwdriver to make a hole at one end of a large honeydew, then a spoon to scoop out the seeds. It took a few attempts but eventually the fit was just right. The wetness. And the post-microwave warmth. Fucking wow. Even one of his young things couldn't compete with that.

After he came, he wiped himself on a dishtowel and put what was left of the melon back in the fridge.

THE WRITER thrust himself against her delicate velvet body and they collided with a violent kiss illuminated by splashes of rainbow-soaked sunshine. Their ribcages knocked together and their ankles collided under dark and distant stars where his body was like the metal of a key: always cold, inflexible, protecting his dilapidating soul from the hollow, wordless comfort of this sad, mad, desperate, lonely world.

THE TEACHER liked it when she came into his room.
She didn't even bother with an excuse and he didn't ask why she was still on school premises so late. Predictably, he was sat reading with a chewed pencil behind his right ear.

'We're leaving,' she said.

He didn't move.

She let out an exaggerated sigh, propping herself up on the table opposite him and swinging her legs impatiently.

'What are you reading?'

No reply.

He tried to ignore her probing but she could see his knuckles turning white.

She started fiddling with the pleats on her dress and whistling, playing up to her part. He looked up at her and stared. His jaw clenched. Her knees went weak.

She grabbed the book from him – something by one of the Beats – and headed for the door. He was quickly out of his chair, as if he'd expected it. He pushed her hard against the wall. She feigned pain. He looked at her, unimpressed, knowing.

He tilted her head up. She started giggling. His expression didn't change. He took the book out of her hand and threw it on the nearest table. She was silent.

They kissed, desperately.

He lifted one of her bare legs and wrapped it around him, slowly sliding a hand up her thigh and pressing his hips into hers. She could feel him, hard, through his suit trousers. As he kissed her neck, she guided her hips to slowly grind herself on him. He responded to every moan and whimper by biting lightly.

He dropped her leg, pushing her aside to pick up his book. Sitting back at his desk he pointed to a spot on the desk with his index finger.

'Here.'

She took a step.

'No,' he said, 'crawl.'

She made her way over to him on hands and knees.

When she reached his desk, he took his cock out and continued reading.

Grabbing the base, she took a saliva-dripping lick up the length of it. He moaned. She teased, licking lightly then pausing to look up from under the table for permission to carry on.

He didn't say anything.

She was sucking desperately fast, twisting her hand and lips around him. He started to thrust, finding the back of her throat. He pulled the back of her hair as he moved her face onto him and was soon enthusiastically fucking her hungry little mouth.

She forced his cock as far as she could down her throat and finally pulled it out, choking, as saliva and semen dripped from both of them.

THE WRITER had already left the exact money on the dresser so she let herself out while he slept.

THE ALCOHOLIC had reached his limits. Physically. Emotionally. Financially. That meant no more money for drink, the one thing he had to have above all others.

Ten years. Ten fucking years of his life, wasted. THE WRITER's manuscript had been sent back by every agent and publisher on his list. They had all said the same thing, as if it was some kind of conspiracy: the only genre he knew how to write wasn't selling. Maybe another time. Maybe not.

Nobody pays for words these days.

Their bodies – the HUSBAND's and the HOOKER's – moved as one toward a rising intensity of primal satisfaction. He knew she was faking it – he'd never been this good, even in his twenties, even when he could still see his dick from a standing position – but he didn't care.

He just wanted to fuck something he wasn't married to, the way she had done.

THE ALCOHOLIC sucked turpentine dregs from plastic bottles, aching for the end of nightmarish day and maybe for the end of it all.

The carpet burns on her knees – the only bare skin visible below the hem of a pleated grey skirt and above white socks – were as fresh as the dark memories of the preceding day's detention. There was also her bruised cervix, but that wouldn't be telling any tales.

BABY GIRL's head hung low under the weight of that term's shame. She had certainly learned a lot in room HE24, but none of it would be of any use when the exams rolled round.

'I handed it in this morning,' she spat out from quivering lips that would shame a whore. 'You know I did, so why do I have to wait behind again?'

THE TEACHER didn't hesitate to slap her across the face. The coarse impact sounded like a hand striking a blackboard.

'Because I say so. That's why. Now get on the fucking desk.'

Unmarked books and used coffee cups were cast aside as BABY GIRL assumed the position; her green eyes fixed on the usual spot on the ceiling. Pens rolled off and landed on the linoleum with a series of small thuds, as heavy as pre-pubescent tears.

THE TEACHER lifted BABY GIRL's legs up and used his callused right hand to hold them there by the slender ankles. The palm of his left hand, with its gold band glistening under the fluorescent bulb, repeatedly spanked the white panties that less than twenty minutes before had been warming a plastic chair over in French.

The grunts of pain were heard as moans of pleasure and it wasn't long before leaden thrusts of a manly pelvis were teaching that sinful little cunt a lesson she'd never forget.

With some money in her purse again, THE HOOKER knew she had to be smart. She had to pay the rent and put some food in the fridge before going anywhere near the coke guy. He was a slippery bastard with long hooks and a bite to go with the bark.

It was late. Dark. The train carriage was deserted, except for her and a man she had never seen before.

Before THE HOOKER realised what was happening, THE JUNKY had grabbed her purse and jumped from the train onto the platform. Seconds later, the doors shut and it began pulling away.

In the early hours of nightmare dawn, THE WRITER pulled his archived sadness down from the dusty top shelf. Too much hard-bitten reality was pressing in from all sides. Not a good idea to verbalise the mood pictures of his mind so he swallowed too many multi-coloured meds and threw his own hurt back at the world by opening his mouth to let out an enormous scream.

Again, no answer. THE HOOKER, who hadn't yet found out her father had hung up forever, didn't know what to do next. With nowhere to go and no idea how to get there, she sat down in the road. Oblivious to the danger, she put her head in her hands and wept.

THE ALCOHOLIC had never been so drunk, nor so desperate to get home. So it was, then, that he fished his keys out of a dark pocket and turned them in the ignition. He soon reached a speed considerably in excess of the legal limit.

Having turned left onto the familiar streets of his own neighbourhood, THE ALCOHOLIC, acting instinctively, swerved to avoid something, or someone.

His car mounted the kerb, where BABY GIRL was nearing her front door on trembling legs.

THE ALCOHOLIC's headlights illuminated a tear-streaked face and small hands scratching at semen-soaked thighs.

Then their worlds went black.

Summer had come to a sudden end, leaving in its wake grey mornings tinged almost imperceptibly with the last remnants of parting sunshine. They sat in idle silence, each lost in a train of private thought. They were content to be there like that, with their daughter's last photograph in a frame between them on the table, and almost twenty minutes passed before a word was spoken. When it came, it was mundane; as if nothing had happened.

'Shall I fix us some coffee?'

THE HUSBAND gave an almost imperceptible nod.
'Sure.'

THE WIFE got up and made her way to the kitchen.

Whisky for Breakfast

I'm in a house I've spent a lot of time in over the years, buttoned into a white shirt that used to fit and a pair of black trousers that never will again. Beside me on the couch is Tommy, my cousin because his absent father was my dead mother's brother. This is the first time we've spoken to each other in nine years. He's showing what I take to be a genuine interest in my public-sector job, unaware I was let go a couple of weeks ago. I don't mention what he does to put food in the freezer because he's a drug dealer who sells industrial quantities of a Tiffany product at Asda prices. He's spent three of the last six years behind the big door and most of his adult life out on bail for one thing or another. Tommy knows I know this but nothing is said. He was to be a tradesman of some kind but, growing up where we did among pish-soaked tenements brimming with junkies and malingerers and half-arsed gangsters, it was never likely to pan out how he wanted. I suppose I was lucky to get away when I did.

When Tommy speaks, I notice his talk is insipid, punctured as it is by generality. He doesn't seem to know a great deal about any one thing, yet this doesn't stop him from offering strong opinions. As we are speaking, his mother, my aunt, puts a plate of food down in front of him.

'Will that hold you, son?' she asks.

'Sure. Thanks.'

'Joseph,' she says, looking at me, 'you want me to fix you something?'

I shake my head. 'No. Thanks, though.'

We are after less than an hour accustomed to the grandfather we shared – dead from heart complications at eighty-one – laid out in an open coffin only a few feet from us. Below a covered mirror, he is looked at and kissed by an impressive procession of mourners whose kind words, however well-intentioned, are cold comfort to me; among them suited men's men wearing grim masks whose broad shoulders will soon be obliged to bear the coffin's leaden weight. He will share his final resting place with an assortment of rosary beads, holy pictures and family mementos. These Irish traditions of familial grief in a confined space have become part of a regular ritual for me in recent years as, one after the other, cancer-ravaged relatives breathed their last. Not so for Tommy, who was away for many of the funerals, following routines of a different kind.

Tommy must have heard me telling an uncle of ours I'm struggling to get by because, at the first lull in conversation, he asks, 'Do you fancy a bit of work, Joseph?'

'I've already got a job, Tommy.'

'I know, but you're short of cash and I thought you might be interested in a wee bit of graft on the side.'

'What kind of work is it?' I ask, although I don't have to and know I shouldn't.

A smirk pulls at the corners of Tommy's mouth. His dark, brooding eyes never leave mine as he pulls a Benson and Hedges out his pack.

After almost a full minute, he says, 'You know the kind. You pick something up in one place then you drive it to another place. You'll get a full envelope for your trouble.'

'Let me think about it, okay?'

'Sure.'

I turn back to look at the corpse of the man who helped raise me, wondering what his advice would be. With tears in my eyes, I realise I'll have to make up my own mind from now on.

Acknowledgements

Some of the stories collected here – in some cases, extracts and earlier versions – were previously published or are scheduled to be published in print or online by *Crooked Holster, Spelk Fiction, Devolution Z, Alternative History Fiction Magazine, Yellow Mama Webzine, Open Pen, Truffle Lit Mag, Potato Soup Journal* and *Glove Lit Zine.* Thank you to all of the editors and readers who saw something of value in the words I put on the page.

I owe a debt of gratitude to Gill James and Debz Hobbs-Wyatt at *Bridge House Publishing.* Debz championed my writing from the very beginning and the stories you've just read are better because of Gill's editorial skills. I'll never forget who gave this book its life in the world. Thank you both. Thank you also to Martin James for his work on the external cover and on the internal images.

Thank you to Jack Kerouac, Charles Bukowski, William Burroughs, Hubert Selby Jr, Raymond Chandler, George V. Higgins, Elmore Leonard, Donald E. Westlake, Jim Thompson, Ernest Hemingway, J.D. Salinger, Richard Matheson, Stephen King, Dennis Lehane, Truman Capote, Hunter S. Thompson, Chuck Palahniuk, Brett Easton Ellis, Irvine Welsh, John Niven, Vladimir Nabokov, James Sallis, Marquis de Sade, Donna Tartt, Martin Booth, Frederick Forsyth, Christopher Hitchens, Gay Talese, Walter Benton, Haruki Murakami and William Shakespeare. I couldn't have written my words without first reading theirs.

Thank you to my colleague and friend, Luigi Coppola, for casting an eye over late drafts of several of these stories. He made numerous great suggestions and the writing is better because of his input. For Luigi's own writing, find him as @MrLuigiCoppola and visit his website: poetrypreacher.com.

Thank you to Vicki Moore (née Buchan) for her words

of praise and encouragement and for her friendship. She and I will eventually collaborate again and I know it will be great because her talent truly is extraordinary. For Vicki's art, find her as @VbArt15 and visit her website: vb-art.co.uk.

Thank you to my English family and friends – especially Dick and Netty, and Rowly and Sarah – for putting their arms around me as one of their own for the best part of twenty years. I appreciated every word, every gesture, and I love you all dearly.

Thank you to The Bhoys and The Uncles – especially Brian, Paddy and Steve – for decades of unbroken love, loyalty and support. Your friendship means everything to me and I don't take it for granted.

Thank you to Laurie and Faye, two incredible women, for showing me that it is possible to emerge – not unscathed, but resolutely unbroken – from even the darkest of days. I am in awe of your fortitude and I love you and your boys – Harris, Max and Leo – very, very much.

Thank you to my Uncle Tam and Aunty Rosie for honouring their sister by loving me like a son. I am grateful for every hug, every kiss, every page of every book. I love you both.

Thank you to you my parents, Pat and Christine, for filling our home with love and books. I'll never be able to adequately express my gratitude.

A special mention to Lucy Ann (Cordery) Mooney: I cherish the precious memories of the eighteen years we spent together and I will always love you '*enough to melt all the tigers of the world to butter.*'

And, finally, to our children – Coco, Otis and Juno: thank you for giving me, every day, the very best of reasons to get up and get on with it. You are amazing, individually and collectively, and I am proud to be your dad. I will never have the words to tell you how much I love you. *I love you.*

About the Author

Christopher P. Mooney was born in Glasgow, Scotland, in 1978. At various times in his life he has been a paperboy, a supermarket cashier, a shelf stacker, a barman, a cinema usher, a carpet-fitter's labourer, a foreign-language assistant and a teacher. He currently lives and writes in someone else's small flat near London. For more of his writing, find him online as @ChrisPatMooney and visit his website: christopherpmooney.com.

Other Publications by Bridge House

Matters of Life and Death

by Philip M Stuckey

Matters of Life and Death is a collection of stories that examines, in different ways, the many insecurities we experience whilst navigating our way towards the inevitable. Whether it is a fear of the unknown, the burden of loss, or the joy of first love, each of us shares a meandering journey of the unexpected that ultimately defines who we are and how we connect with the universe that created us.

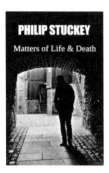

"Varied, deep and interesting, I enjoyed every story. Highly recommended." (*Amazon*)

Order from Amazon:

Paperback: ISBN 978-1-907335-85-3
eBook: ISBN 978-1-907335-86-0

Drawn by the Sea

by Jeanne Davies

You will find in this collection a mixture of themes and genres. There are brushes with the supernatural, an exploration of human emotions, history, love and loss, and also a firm sense of time and place.

Jeanne Davies thinks up her stories whilst walking for miles in the countryside with her Labrador companion at her side. Wandering along the seashore with the serenity and chaos of the ocean inspires and gives her peace.

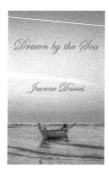

"The stories are intriguing, clever and written so beautifully you feel completely immersed. Great read!" (*Amazon*)

Order from Amazon:

Paperback: ISBN 978-1-907335-82-2
eBook: ISBN 978-1-907335-83-9

Days Pass like a Shadow

by Paula R.C. Readman

Within the pages of *Days Pass like a Shadow* are thirteen dark
tales covering the theme of death and loss. At the centre of
every story is a beating heart. For the reader to make the
journey to that centre, along the flowing veins of the words, all
they need is a few minutes during a lunch break, or at the end
of the day. The reader will be introduced to a rich and diverse
collection of characters - a gardener, a serial killer, a time
traveller, a sleepwalker and many more.

"Thirteen very different stories, each in its own time and
location, but all connected by death and loss. There is
something here for everyone. I enjoyed each and every story.
You are pulled in from the very first word." (*Amazon*)

Order from Amazon:

Paperback: ISBN 978-1-907335-80-8
eBook: ISBN 978-1-907335-81-5